I0529685

SOMEONE TO LOVE

BY

DAWN SCALA

WOLFCLOUD BOOKS
HARVARD, IL

Someone To Love

Copyright @ 1998 by Dawn Scala

All rights reserved. No part of this book may be used or reproduced in any manner, including photocopying, whatsoever without written permission except in the case of brief quotations embodied in critical articles and reviews. Published in the United States by Wolfcloud Books.

Printed in the United States of America

Someone to Love / Dawn Scala

ISBN 0-615-12441-0

Edited by Patricia Farley
Book cover design by Keith Seda

Warning Disclaimer

This novel is fiction. Places, names, characters, and incidents are the product of the author's imagination or are used fictitiously. Any resemblance to actual events or locales or persons, living or dead, is entirely coincidental.

SOMEONE TO LOVE

To my dear friend Patti, thank you for always being there for me no matter what.

WOLFCLOUD BOOKS

SOMEONE TO LOVE

Chapter one

Connie sat on the living room floor in her white flannel pajamas staring at the top of the Christmas tree. "Mom, I think we need another star," she yelled. "This one looks old."

"I'll pick up another one when we're out." Connie's mother appeared from the hallway wearing her red winter coat and pulling her white scarf around her neck. "Don't expect us back for a couple of hours. I'm sure the stores will be packed with holiday shoppers."

"Okay Mom," Connie said. She watched her mom make a final inspection in the hallway mirror. Connie had inherited her mother's beautiful features. Her long silky black hair, her creamy complexion, and her crystal blue eyes. Connie liked the way her mother's red coat brought out the rose colored blush she always wore. The car horn beeped from outside the house.

"I'd better get out there before your father gets upset."

Connie's mother grabbed her purse from a nearby chair and turned to Connie and smiled.

"Don't forget to pick up that sweater I saw for dad. I know he was hinting last time we were there." Connie said with a smile.

"I'll do my best." Connie's mother walked over to her daughter and kissed her on the cheek. "Be good."

Connie turned her attention back to the Christmas tree for a final inspection. It was beautiful, she thought. The smell of pine filled the room. Her father always insisted on real trees. She watched as the lights twinkled. As far back as she could remember they always put the tree in the same corner of the huge living room with its cathedral ceiling. This way the tree could be seen from the outside as you pulled up to the front of the house. Connie reached over to the coffee table and grabbed the remote and turned on the T.V.

Chapter two

"Do you think we bought out the mall?" Bill teased his wife as he closed the trunk to the car.

"Very funny," Catherine said smiling. "Connie will be so thrilled this year; I can't wait."

"You spoil her every year." Bill opened the passenger side for his wife and then quickly got in behind the wheel. "It's really starting to get cold with that wind. I think I'll get a fire going when we get home." Bill moved his hand to Catherine's and squeezed. They turned out onto the main highway and headed home. It was a forty-minute drive that mainly consisted of farms. Bill took his hand from Catherine's and turned on the radio. He went through a few channels before he found one that he liked. When his eyes returned to the road he quickly grabbed the steering wheel with both hands.

"What the hell is wrong with that guy?" Bill said as he watched a semi swerving toward them. "Oh God, it's coming right at us." He quickly hit the brake with his foot and turned the wheel hoping to avoid the huge semi, but instead the car swerved in front of it. He could hear Catherine's screams being drowned out by the metal tearing apart the car that encased them. His last thoughts were of their sweet twelve years old daughter, Connie, at home decorating the tree.

Chapter three

The ring of the doorbell woke Connie. Sleepily, she looked at the clock on the mantle. It was twelve thirty. Why did Mom not wake me, she thought. The doorbell rang again and a sinking feeling came over Connie as she saw the flashing red lights through the sheer curtains. She opened the door to see two police officers. Connie's heart began to pound.

"Is there anyone here that we can talk to?" He said, looking very sad.

Connie shook her head as the two men looked at each other. The one police officer bent down to her.

"Honey, is there anyone we can call for you?"

Connie began to cry, and nodded. "My best friend, Loretta." She led the two officers to the phone and dialed the number. One of the men took the phone from her hand and the other led Connie into the kitchen. She tried to hear what he was saying but his voice was very low.

"What is your name?" said the young looking officer. "Connie," she replied. "Something's happened to my parents, hasn't it?"

"Connie, come here and sit down."

Connie walked over to one of the stools that lined the counter and sat as she was told of her parent's fate. The officer took a long time before he spoke.

"Honey, there was bad car accident," he hesitated. "And your parents were sent to the hospital."

Connie sat silently overcome by fear and sadness. Her whole body felt numb. She heard voices in the hallway and looked up to see Loretta's mother and father coming towards her.

"Oh, my dear," Loretta's mother said with tears streaking down her face. She put her arms around Connie and held her close. "We'll take care of you, darling; you're coming home with us."

Connie looked up into her tear-streaked face. She noticed her hair was in disarray. "My parents are at the hospital; I want to go see them now" she insisted.

Loretta's mother looked over to the police officers with confusion.

"Ma'am, may I talk to you privately?" The officer followed her into the living room. "I am so sorry," he said, distraught. "I told her they were in the hospital. I thought it would be better hearing it from someone she knew rather than a total stranger. It's going to be something she'll remember the rest of her life."

Chapter four

Loretta's parents handled the funeral arrangements and made the decision to take Connie in as their own. Mary was Connie's mother's best friend through high school. When Connie was born she asked her to be her godmother. Connie had become very sullen and distraught. She hardly spoke to anyone.

The day of the funeral, Loretta's father had to drive by the scene of the accident. Skid marks from both vehicles were still on the road. "Please stop the car." Connie insisted. Not far from the road she spotted something and quickly got out and ran toward it. Her heart broke in two as she discovered it was the sweater she asked her mom to buy for her dad. She wished they had not stopped. Connie broke into uncontrollable sobs and felt Loretta's mom, Mary, at her side holding her as she wept.

Chapter five

Connie later learned the truck driver had fallen asleep at the wheel when he plowed into her parents car. It was proven later in court that the driver, who lived with minimal injuries, had too many hours on the road without sleep. Mary explained to Connie that the lawyer that handled her parents will thought it would be in her best interest to pursue a lawsuit. An out of court settlement had given her a substantial amount of money, which was put into a trust for her along with her parent's modest size home, until she turned eighteen.

As years passed, Connie's pain began to fade. Although now she felt like part of the family, Christmas would always send her into a deep depression. She tried to hide her feelings, but Mary somehow knew and would come up and hug her without saying a word.

Chapter six

The gold antique clock that sat on the mantle read twelve thirty. Connie quickly ran around the living room looking under newspapers, pillows, and furniture--anywhere her one boot could have crawled. It was always that one black boot that simply vanished into thin air. Should I give up and wear another pair? No, I will find it, and so what if I am late? He will forgive me. Connie thought of Rick. He had called and told her to come over at one o'clock. From his house they would drive up to the Rocking K and go horseback riding. The horse ranch they were going to was beautiful, Connie thought. It was set in the hills and surrounded by a thick forest. Some of the trails led to ponds and others led to open pastures. Connie knew them all. She had met Rick there two years ago and since then they would often go there on weekends. She remembered how her pulse raced the first time she laid eyes on him as he sat high on the black stallion he was riding. His complexion, darkened by the sun, seemed clean-shaven and smooth to the touch. His eyes, dark but soft, were enhanced by his long black eye lashes. His nose and chin gave people the impression he was a strong person. Someone you could trust. His lips--she loved kissing his lips. Ah, there! She saw the tip of her black boot peeking out at her from under the side of the recliner. She quickly grabbed it before it could get away again and slipped it on her foot. All she needed was her brush. Forget it; she decided that would take another half an hour to find. Instead, she ran her fingers through her silky long dark hair. Connie took a final look at herself in the hallway mirror that hung on the wall. Her crystal blue eyes smiled back. "You look great." She grabbed her purse and her keys, double locked the door behind her, and headed toward her black Camaro. She was glad she did not run into any of her neighbors. She would then have to chitchat, and she was running late as it was. She started her car and was on her way. It was a going to be a beautiful night tonight. The skies so clear you could see the stars. The temperature was not too warm. Connie continued out of the little town where she was raised. She expected to grow old here as well. Just like Mrs. Evans, who owned the bakery in town. Connie would go in every Friday morning and buy Mrs. Evans' freshly baked long johns. Mrs. Evans would tell her customers how she grew up in the small town of Greenville and married Mr. Evans, who passed away seven years ago. She was alone now. She and Mr. Evans were never able to have children. Everyone knew everyone in this quaint little town. When Connie's parents passed away a few years back in the accident, it seemed the whole town showed their concern for her. Being an only child, Connie appreciated it. She passed the rolling hills that surrounded and protected the little town and drove through the open land that held farms and cattle ranches. Rick lived in an apartment in the next town. She turned off the car and walked into his place. She knew she would find him sitting on the couch watching television.

"Hi babe," Rick stood up and walked over to Connie and kissed her gently on her lips. "Mmm, you taste good. Strawberry lipstick?" He kissed her again and held her close. He breathed in deep, smelling the sweetness of her perfume that she wore and kissed her neck.

Connie moaned, feeling Rick's hardness as he pressed against her. She felt his hands reaching under her shirt to undo her bra and his fingers gently touching her firm breasts. Connie gasped. He picked her up and carried her into the bedroom, laying her gently on his bed. They quickly undressed. Rick stood over her and watched as she breathed with anticipation. Connie knew he could hold back no longer as he climbed on top of her, kissing her breasts, then her lips. She eagerly arched her back as he entered her. After he came, Rick lay next to her. Connie waited for Rick to fall asleep, then quietly slipped out of the bed and into the washroom, where she could satisfy the excitement Rick had started in her. She then washed herself and went back into the bedroom and got dressed.

"Rick," she nudged him, "wake up, and let's go."

He grabbed her arm and pulled her toward him, kissing

her. "Do you really feel like riding today?"

"Yes, now let's go." She urged.

"Okay, Okay," Rick smiled as he grabbed his jeans off the floor and proceeded to dress. "But I'm driving. You drive too fast."

"So, you do not like my driving?" Connie knew her driving made Rick nervous. "I like to go fast, especially when riding. It makes me feel so free, so wild, so alive!" Connie waved her arms in the air. It was a high nothing else could compare to, she thought. In that respect, she and Rick were totally opposite. As she watched him put on his boots she thought how sensible and predictable he was.

As they pulled up at the ranch, Connie watched Gus, who owned the Rocking K, wave and walk inside the barn. He soon appeared with the two horses bridled and ready to go.

"Thanks, Gus," Connie said, taking the reins from his hand.

"You know missy," he said, winking at Connie. "I had me a feeling you two were coming today. It's a beautiful day, isn't it?"

"It sure is," Connie said as she put her left foot in the stirrup to mount. Once seated, she looked over at Rick who was also ready. "We'll see you in awhile, Gus." She watched him smile and disappear back into the barn. Connie led her horse first and Rick followed behind her. She decided to take the path that wound up around the highest hill. They had not taken this trail since the previous fall. With winter ending two months ago, the ground had been too wet and made it easy to slide down into one of the gullies. Today, Connie thought, the ground looked dry. She slowed down noticing the many branches that had grown over on to the path. A few of them scraped Connie's arm. "I'll have to tell Gus he needs to get some of these branches cut." Connie yelled back to Rick. Finally they came to a clearing. Connie stopped to wait for Rick to come up beside her.

"The winner pays for dinner." Rick's eyes teased.

"No, no, it's the loser that buys," she said triumphantly. "You're just saying that 'cause you know I always win."

"We'll see about that." Rick kicked in his heels and the horse sped off ahead of Connie.

Connie was quick to follow. Her long dark hair, blowing in the wind, caught up to Rick. "That's not fair," she laughed. She then nudged her horse to go faster, leaving Rick in a dusty trail. As she neared the end of the pasture she slowed down to a trot. Behind her, she heard Rick's horse squeal. When she turned, she saw Rick's horse with its front hooves in the air. She watched as Rick's eyes widened with fear as he fell to the ground.

"Oh Rick, are you okay?" She quickly dismounted and ran to his side.

"I think so," he said, rubbing his leg. He moved it to see if it felt broken. "She must have slid or something; I'm Okay." Rick stood up with the help of Connie. He walked over to the horse and petted her nose. "What happened girl?" He checked out her hooves and ran his hand down her legs. When convinced she seemed fine, he mounted her.

Connie let out a sigh of relief. "You scared me," she laughed, feeling the tension subside. "You should have seen your face." She got back up on her horse and this time followed Rick back to the ranch.

"You two were not out for very long." Gus said, scratching his head.

"Oh Rick had a little mishap," Connie teased. "I think he purposely fell thinking I'd feel sorry for him and buy dinner."

"Are you all right Rick?" Gus asked, concerned.

"I will be fine, Gus," Rick said as he rubbed his behind. "We will see you in a couple of weeks," he said as he put his arm around Connie. "You are not buying me dinner," he teased as he gently squeezed her arm. "You're so cruel to me."

Connie reached behind Rick and swatted him hard on his behind.

"Ouch," he yelled. "I'm real tender there right now." They drove back to Rick's and ordered a pizza and watched TV until one in the morning, then headed for bed.

Connie smiled, "can we go to Loretta's next week? She asked if we could stop by and visit." Loretta was still her best friend. They were like sisters since Loretta's family took her in on that fateful night; the night she was home waiting for her parents to return from Christmas shopping. The memory of that horrible night still haunted her. The police officers coming to the door, Loretta's mom crying as she told her that her parents were killed. Connie found out later that Christmas presents for her were found in the road.

Chapter seven

Rick finished drinking his coffee and put the empty cup in the sink. He grabbed his keys, locked the door behind him and headed toward his car. Another long grueling week, he thought as he headed out of town. He worked an average of fifty hours a week at Carson's, one of the largest corporations in the United States. They manufactured cellular phones, among other communication products. Rick's job was to keep in contact with customers and if they felt dissatisfied for any reason, resolve it. The end of the month he would give his report to the division and tell them how well they did on making their quota. His job paid very well, and Rick was good at it. He considered himself very lucky to be in that position, for only being twenty-six. Right after high school he had started college and earned a bachelor's degree in business. His father's friend helped him get the job at Carson's. He soon realized he had a knack for pleasing people. So did Carson's; which is why they promoted him shortly after he was hired. When the weekends came he just wanted to be with Connie. Many of their friends would go out to bars, get drunk and make total fools of themselves. He was not into alcohol and being around people who had too much to drink made him feel uncomfortable. Connie, on the other hand, was different. When she drank, he could not wait to get her into bed. She would go wild.

"Hi Rick, how was your weekend?" Sally asked as he entered the office.

"Fine, how was yours?" Rick sat down at his desk next to Sally's and yawned. He noticed the way she smiled at him as she tapped her long red fingernails on the desk. "Okay, what is it? I can tell you're dying to tell me something."

"Hey, lover boy" Sally teased, "you better wake up for this one. We are having a meeting in fifteen minutes. The rumor is..." she looked around to see if anyone was listening, "...they're opening another plant down south and looking to send someone there to get things started. Of course we're talking months away, but who do you think they'll ask?"

Rick shrugged his shoulders, "Bob, probably, he has been with the company for a long time."

"I don't think so," Sally stopped in the middle of her sentence. She noticed their boss, Mr. Sanders, walking towards them.

"Come on you two," he said as he motioned Sally and Rick to follow him into the meeting room. "Let's get this day started."

Rick took a seat at the long table and watched as Mr. Sanders took his place at the head. As usual, he dressed nice, but causal. He wore a white shirt with thin red pin stripes and black pants. Up until five years ago, the company required all managers to wear a tie. Then a drastic change took place. The vice president felt since the company sold communications products, all employees should have good communication skills. In helping to achieve this goal, the company sent the workers to school to learn proper English and writing skills. Another change was to make all workers feel equal and to bridge the gap between managers and the rest of the employees. In doing so, the managers were no longer required to adhere to the dress code.

"I suppose you've all heard the rumor that's been going around." Mr. Sanders watched the eager faces that sat watching him. "It is true that we will be opening another plant in Champaign. And it is also true we will be trying to decide who we want down there to get the ball rolling. I do not have to tell you the company is willing to pay the people that go a huge salary increase plus moving expenses. And I also know that not all of you are going to want to move." His eyes rested on Sally before continuing. "We realize some of you have children and have put down roots in the community. Our intention is not to disrupt any families." Mr. Sanders watched the tension leave Sally's face. "We'll let you know more as things come up. But for now, if there aren't any questions, let's get to work."

"Well, Rick, what do you think?" Sally asked once they were clear of anyone hearing. "Do you think you would want to move down to Champaign?"

"I don't know Sally. Let's see who they want down there first."

Chapter eight

Rick opened the door for Connie as they entered the restaurant they went to every Sunday morning. The place, crowded with churchgoers, seemed happy the sermon did not take that long today. Some of the patrons Rick and Connie knew smiled and waved. It was hard to go anywhere without recognizing someone. Pat brought their food and filled their coffee cups. "Will there be anything else?"

"No thanks, Pat," Rick said with a smile. She quickly wrote out the bill and continued on to another table. "So, what should we do today?" Rick asked. He noticed how the sun shinning through the window cast a warm glow across Connie's face, making her more beautiful than she already was--if that were possible. Although he knew he was very handsome and probably could have any girl he wanted, he felt honored she had chosen him to love.

Connie smiled, "Can we go to Loretta's, she asked if we

could stop by and visit?" Loretta was her best friend. They grew up together. He knew how close Connie and Loretta were, and he liked Loretta. She was a good person; one who would say exactly what was on her mind. They paid the bill and headed toward Greenville. Loretta rented a town home a few blocks away from Connie. It was a nice area and every other house seemed to have kids. He spotted the familiar car in her driveway and pulled behind it. "Well it looks like she's home."

"Hi Rick, Connie, how is it going?" Loretta greeted them with a hug. "Come in and sit, you want something to drink? I have some wine." Loretta stood in the middle of her living room. She prided herself with the way it looked, very modern. She had chosen every piece of furniture and wall hangings, and for the most part was pleased. She brushed a strand of her fine red hair from her face.

"Wine is fine," Connie said sitting back on the couch. She watched her friend go into the other room and quickly returned with two cold glasses and set the bottle down on the table. Connie grabbed two coasters that were nearby. "I know how you feel about ring marks," she teased. "Would you believe little things like that could start fights between us?"

"But we always make up," Loretta added. "We could never stay mad at one another for very long." Loretta sat across from them and took a sip of her wine. "Sam is having a party next weekend. It's his birthday, and you two should come. Do you know it will be seven months I have been seeing him? I think I have broken my record. Maybe

I have finally found the person who can tolerate my arrogant behavior."

"I think the word you're looking for is eccentric," Connie teased. "And you know perfectly well, nine times out of ten you're the one that breaks off with a guy. What was the name of the one that was stalking you?"

"He was not stalking me." Loretta insisted, as she waved her arm through the air, indicating Connie was exaggerating. "He was just infatuated, that's all. He was perfectly harmless."

"Perfectly harmless men don't wait outside your door numerous nights in a row and scream obscenities for the whole town to hear." Connie poured herself another glass of wine and turned toward Rick. "Did I tell you about that one?"

"Yes, but my personal favorite was the one that ordered all those black roses when you told him it was over. I do not always enjoy talking about her various boyfriends. "I guess we can come to Sam's party."

"Great." Loretta grabbed some paper from a nearby table and jotted down the address and directions to Sam's house. "Be there about seven; I'm glad both of you are coming. I don't know too many of his friends." She finished writing and handed the slip to Connie. "I still haven't found him a present. Can you go shopping with me later this week, Connie? You always seem to know what to buy for Rick."

"Sure," Wednesday night is good for me. We can go to the mall; they have a lot of men's stores to choose from." Connie finished her glass of wine and stood up to leave.

"We'd better get going. I have things to do. I will call you tomorrow," Connie said, as she and Rick turned to leave.

It was early evening by the time they got back to his place. He knew Connie was feeling tipsy from the wine. He let her lead him by the hand into the bedroom and watched as she slowly undressed. The hunger showing in her eyes as she caressed her own breasts and then slowly moved her hands down between her legs, Rick felt himself becoming excited as he heard Connie moan. He quickly undressed and took her into his arms and kissed her passionately. Leaving a wet trail to where her hands were, he then picked her up and laid her gently on the bed as she spread her legs and waited for him to enter.

Chapter nine

The week started out the same as always for Connie. Monday she went into the Local Press, where she worked. It was a small newspaper that listed what was on sale at the grocery store and where to go for garage sales. It also gave current information on what was going on around town. Connie would take down the information and give it to the editor, Jim. The pay was not much, but Connie was financially secure from the lawsuit that involved her parent's death and their estate. She liked working for Jim. He was an easygoing guy that did not complain if she took a day off or came in late. Connie was hired to take Jim's wife, Betsy's place when she became pregnant with their second child. Occasionally she would come in and check on Connie to see how she was doing. Connie did not mind; she would have questions that Jim could not answer. Tuesday after work, she stopped at the local hot-dog stand to grab something to eat. She felt starved; she had skipped lunch that day. The phone had been ringing constantly. People called wanting to place ads for their garage sales. It seemed as if the whole town was having one in two weeks. As she entered the kitchen, Misty, her cat, came running up to greet her. Connie set the brown paper bag on the kitchen counter and bent down to pick her up in her arms. "You smell my food. Let's see what we have for you." Connie set Misty down and looked in the cabinet where she had several cans of cat food. "How about some Tuna?" She pulled back the tab and tossed it in the garbage, grabbed a spoon from the nearby drawer, and scooped it into Misty's dish. The cat eagerly chewed down her food. Connie grabbed a plate for herself and placed the hot-dog and fries on it. She took her food into the living room and sat on the couch. She grabbed the remote and flipped on the television. Old reruns were her favorite to watch this time of the day. She had finished her dinner when the phone rang. She knew before picking it up that it was Rick. He called her every day about this time.

"Connie, it doesn't look like I can go to the party this weekend. A problem came up with a customer and I have to go out of town."

Connie did not try to hide her disappointment. "Rick, I'm not going if you cannot go. I'll call and tell Loretta we can't make it."

Rick fell silent a few seconds. "Look, I think you should go. It is not fair for you to sit home just because I have to work. Besides, Loretta will be upset."

"I won't know anyone there. I'm not going; I'll feel too uncomfortable," Connie stated in a flat tone to Rick, letting him know he should not pursue the matter any further. "Besides, there are things around here I've been meaning to do and I've been lazy. I can get started on painting my bathroom, or clean out my closets. Believe me, it's better this way."

"Well, at least I won't have to worry about you. You better call Loretta soon as possible to let her know."

Their conversation turned to the day's events and Rick promised to call her soon as he came back. She hung up the phone feeling relieved it did not turn into a huge argument. If she wanted to stay home, that was her decision. He will only be gone three short days and then he will be with her again.

When he came back she would cook him a romantic dinner with candles and wine. They would then sit in front of the fireplace and make love. She would show Rick how much she missed him.

Connie decided to wait till the next evening to tell Loretta. They had planned to go shopping; and it could wait. She knew her friend would try to talk her into going. She really had no intentions of going if Rick was not going to attend. She also knew how insistent Loretta could be. Maybe she would wait until the last minute and pretend she was sick. Either way, Loretta would be angry. Maybe I will go, she thought, and only stay for fifteen minutes and then say I am sick. Connie thought about it the rest of the night. Which would be worse, going to a party where you did not know anyone, or facing Loretta?

The next evening when Connie came home, there was a message on her machine from Loretta reminding her that they were going shopping, and to call her soon as she got home. Connie fixed herself a cold glass of ice tea before picking up her phone. "I will pick you up and we can grab something to eat at the mall," Connie suggested. "Just give me about twenty minutes to change and feed Misty."

"That sounds good. I have to throw some things in the wash and I should be ready when you pull into the driveway."

Connie hung up with her friend and flew up the stairs to her bedroom. She had kept her room, though her parent's room was much larger and provided a master washroom. She looked around at the disarray of clothes thrown everywhere. On one side of the room laid a pile of clean clothes. On the other side laid the dirty pile. It is no wonder Rick never liked to spend the weekends at her home she thought, the whole house was a mess. One of these days I will make the effort to become organized. Connie quickly went to the clean pile of clothes and grabbed a pair of jeans and a t-shirt. She pulled her long hair out from the shirt, ran a quick brush through it, grabbed her shoes, and went back down the stairs to feed her cat. In a few minutes she was on her way to Loretta's. When she pulled into the driveway, Connie honked. Her friend emerged from the town home, locked the door, and got in on the passenger's side.

"God, how much perfume do you need?" Connie quickly

rolled down her window. The sweet odor was so strong it made Connie's eyes water. "What is your intention, to attract the opposite sex or keep them at bay?"

"I'm sorry," Loretta giggled. "I didn't have time to take a shower this morning so I thought I could wear extra perfume just in case. I did not realize I had put so much on. No wonder everyone was giving me strange looks today at work. Let's eat at the burger place," Loretta suggested once they walked into the mall. It was a good time to be there, the place was half empty and they found a table right away. The waitress came and took their order and returned shortly with their dinner.

"About the party," Connie started to say after taking a sip of her coke. "Rick has to go out of town and…" Connie noticed the glare coming into Loretta's eyes. Oh hell, she thought. This will turn into a big fight if I do not go. "…and I probably will not stay long." A look of relief came across Loretta's face.

"I thought you were going to tell me you weren't going to go. Do not worry; I will stay with you at the party. I know how it can be when you do not know anyone. You'll have a good time, wait and see."

Connie felt a little better upon hearing that. Though she still was not thrilled about going without Rick, she felt committed now. After they finished eating, they paid the bill and proceeded to find Sam a present. They had gone into several men's stores before Loretta found something she liked. A long light gray robe made out of satin.

"I will enjoy this," Loretta cooed as she ran her hand along the soft material. "What do you think? He'll look great in it." They walked up to the check out where a good-looking guy took the garment from Loretta's hand.

"Will there be anything else?" He asked, as he rang up the total and placed the robe in a bag.

"Yes," Loretta lured with her eyes, "my place tonight at seven."

Connie watched as the young man blushed. She knew Loretta loved teasing guys. It seemed so much fun for her. Most of them never knew how to take it. Connie laughed, "Please excuse my friend; she is deranged." The expression on the young man's face was pure shock and embarrassment at first. He then regained control and smiled. It was obvious, Connie thought, even though he was only nineteen or twenty, he knew how good looking he was, and had similar encounters from other women. "Well, I'm sure you made his day." Connie remarked once they were out of the store.

Loretta licked her lips. I would not mind running into him again, when he is about seven years older. Oh well, let's head for home, it's almost nine and the stores will be closing soon." Connie agreed and they headed out of the mall. "I'm really glad you're coming to Sam's party. How about you following me there Saturday and you can help set things up? You know, put out the paper plates and cups, things like that."

Connie agreed, "Call me when you decide what time you want to be there." She pulled into her friend's driveway and Loretta grabbed her present and her purse and got out of the car.

"Thanks for going with me. I'll talk to you soon. Good night." She closed the car door and walked up to her door with her house keys in her hand. She turned and waved one more time before going in the house.

When Connie came home, she found there was a message from Rick on her machine asking her to call. She settled on her couch and dialed the familiar number. As she waited for him to pick up, Misty jumped up and snuggled in her lap. Purring for attention, Connie began to pet her soft fur.

"So, what kind of trouble did Loretta get herself into tonight?" Rick teased, knowing Connie was with her friend when she did not answer the phone.

"Oh, the usual, trying to abduct young and innocent men to control and sacrifice for her own selfish needs." She waited for Rick's laughter to subside. "I'm going with her to Sam's party; it will cause a fight if I don't go. I wish you could go with me," she added.

"Oh," Rick said hesitantly. "I understand. You should go, she's your friend. I only wish I could go with you, but this is my job, this is what I do. And it's very rare that they send me out of town like this."

"I know, I know," Connie said sadly. "Call me as soon as you get back."

"I will," Rick assured her. "I'll think about you the whole time I'm gone, I promise. We will make it a special night when I get back. I'll show you how much I missed you, still my girl?"

"Forever and ever," Connie replied. She knew she would not hear from him until the following Wednesday. His plane left tomorrow at noon and there would be no time before that for him to call. Rick still had some packing to do, so she said good-bye. Connie felt a strange ache in her heart, as she replaced the receiver. Somehow she knew things would never be the same between them as they were right now. The feeling stayed with her the rest of the evening. As she drifted off to sleep, she dreamed that she was falling and suddenly Rick's face appeared and she reached out to grasp his outstretched hand. Just as she was about to grab onto him, he pulled away. Connie awoke abruptly, perspiration running down her back, her heart pounding wildly. Misty jumped up next to her sensing something was wrong. "What was that all about?" She lay in bed for a while with her eyes wide-open waiting for her heart to slow down to normal. It was sometime after two before sleep came to her again.

Chapter ten

Connie knew Loretta planned to spend the night at Sam's. It was best if she followed her there, she thought. That way she could leave when she wanted. It was about five-thirty when they arrived with a bag of goodies. Potato chips, beer, pop, paper plates, anything they could think of to bring. Sam greeted Loretta with a kiss and followed the girls into the kitchen. They proceeded to take the items out of the bags and set them on the table.

"Please hand me a beer," Loretta said to Connie, who was busy putting the items in the refrigerator. She grabbed the beer and popped open the tab. Then she leaned against the counter. "How many people are coming tonight?"

Sam shrugged his shoulders, "I invited some people from work and they said they would come, and then there is Tony and a few of the couples we have double dated with. Total, I would say about fifteen to twenty people will probably show. I am sorry Rick could not make it," he turned his attention to

Connie. "Loretta said he had to go out of town on business. Well, I'm glad you came," Sam smiled as he put his arm around Loretta's waist.

Connie returned the smile. Thanks." She began feeling a little less uncomfortable. Just then, the doorbell rang and Sam quickly went to answer it. Connie and Loretta remained in the kitchen and could hear several voices entering the apartment. A few walked into the kitchen asking where the drinks were. Upon seeing the variety of alcohol, a man that was medium height with sandy colored hair and glasses started to check out the selection.

"What should I start out with?" he said picking up a bottle of Brandy. "Is there any orange juice?" He asked Connie, who was standing next to the refrigerator. Noticing the strange expression on her face he quickly apologized. "I'm sorry, how rude of me, my name is Burt. I'm a friend of Sam's, and you must be?"

"Connie," she answered, opening the door to see if there was any orange juice. She spotted a container way in the back and handed it to Burt. "If I were you, I'd smell it to see if it's still good."

"It should be," Sam boasted as he entered the room. "I just bought it two days ago. Are you trying to scare off guests before this party even starts?" Sam teased. "You better keep an eye on her, Loretta," he said pointing a finger at her. "She'll have everyone thinking they're going home with botulism."

"That very well may be the truth," Loretta waived her index finger back at him, smiling. "I've seen what is growing under your peas and carrots that you keep in the vegetable drawer. It's not a pretty sight, folks."

Burt laughed as he took a sip of his drink. "Gee, Loretta, tell us more. We all thought we knew our old buddy Sam. To find out something like this makes me feel even closer to him. Is there anything we should know about his underwear drawer?"

Everyone laughed, and Connie grabbed another beer. She heard the doorbell ring and this time someone from the living room answered it. More people entered the kitchen and now the room was getting thick with cigarette smoke. She could not stand the smell and walked into the living room. There were a lot of people there too, but at least she could breathe easier. She did not see a place to sit, so she stayed by the door. Everyone paired off in groups, engrossed in conversation. Connie could only hear bits and pieces before the volume of someone's laughter drowned out what she heard. She decided she would have another beer and leave. She knew Loretta would try to change her mind. Connie finished her beer and turned abruptly, almost walking into someone. "Oh, I'm sorry; I didn't know you were there." She stepped back to give the man some space and looked into the bluest eyes she had ever seen. Connie felt as she was going to melt. He was the most handsome man she ever encountered. His shoulder length blonde hair, parted down the middle, was soft and neatly combed back off his forehead. He wore a loose fitting black sweatshirt with a university logo on the front."

"That's all right; there isn't enough room in this place for

all these people. I was just about to step outside for some
fresh air. Care to join me?"

Connie hesitated. "Well, I was on my way into the kitchen
to get another beer." Just then, someone walking by bumped
her, knocking her closer again into this handsome man.
Connie felt a strange electrical charge go between them and
wondered if he also felt it. She looked up into his blue eyes
that were now smiling at her. There were no telltale signs
that he felt it too, and Connie thought it was perhaps her
imagination playing tricks on her.

"Stay right here," he said, taking her plastic cup from her
hand. "I'll get it for you. If I let you go in there I might
never see you again." He turned and pushed his way
through the crowd toward the kitchen.

Connie smiled as she leaned against the wall. She might
find this party interesting after all. A few minutes later, she
spotted him on his way back with a beer in each hand.
When he reached her, she opened the front door and both
exited out the door. Once outside, the warm fresh air felt
good. Connie brushed a strand of hair away from her face
before taking the beer from his hand. She then took a sip.
"I'm Connie, a friend of Loretta's."

"I'm Tony, a friend of Sam's. You look familiar to me. I
think I've met you before." Tony raised his eyebrows, "I'm
trying to remember where I've seen you, but nothing is
popping into my mind. Where do you live?"

"Greenville," Connie answered. She could not help
noticing how handsome he was as the sunset cast a reddish-
orange glow in the sky behind him. This man surely must

belong to someone, she thought. She was sure he had come to the party alone. "Perhaps we met at another party?" But Connie knew if she had, she would have remembered him.

"Maybe," he answered. "It will come to me later. What counts, is that I know you now." Tony gave her a warm smile.

Connie learned that Tony was six years older than her and lived two towns over from Greenville. Aside from being a construction worker he played guitar in a local band. Tony seemed surprised when Connie did not recognize the name of the band, the "Quick Shots." He went on to tell her about the guys he played with and how everyone seemed to like them. They were planning to go into a studio to produce their songs. From there they would send out demos to recording agencies. Connie felt fascinated by what Tony was telling her. She could see his eyes sparkle with excitement as he told her his dreams of one day being signed by a big record company.

Tony noticed Connie had finished her cup and took it from her hand. "Do not go anywhere," he said. A few minutes later he returned with two more beers. He sat on the sidewalk beside her. "I'm sorry, I've been going on and on about me. I really would like to know about you."

Connie went on to tell him about how her parent's died and that she went to live with Loretta's parents until the age of nineteen.

Suddenly, Tony gasped, "I remember reading about the incident in the paper. It was an article on truck drivers falling asleep behind the wheel, and there was a recent interview with you on your feelings about it. The paper showed your picture and I remember thinking how beautiful this girl is and how sad it must be to lose your parents when you're just a kid. The memory of it must come back to you every Christmas."

Connie usually never liked talking about it; it made her sad to think about her parents. But this time she did not feel that way. Maybe it was the way Tony made her feel comfortable. Or maybe it was the beer. "I did the article for the paper a few months ago," she said.

"Only because Jim, my boss, thought it would benefit the issue." She realized she must be getting drunk, she would not be pouring out her feelings like this. She looked up and saw a tall blonde with huge boobs heading toward them.

"Tony, I've been trying to get your attention all night. Where is your band playing next?" The girl asked, crouching very close to Tony. She had one hand resting on his shoulder and the other holding a beer. She looked over at Connie and smiled. Connie smiled back, but felt uncomfortable. This girl obviously knew Tony very well. She sat and listened quietly as the two of them discussed the band and people Connie never heard of before. Soon Tony realized the girls did not know each other and introduced the two. Connie learned the girl with the big boobs name was Angie. A few minutes later, some more people gathered around them. Someone mentioned there were too many people inside Sam's. Fifteen minutes passed, and Connie turned to Tony and asked if he knew what time it was.

He looked at his watch. "It's almost midnight. I am sorry, I've been ignoring you." He gently put his hand on hers and leaned over to whisper into her ear. "You're not thinking of leaving me, are you?"

Connie felt that same electrical charge she had earlier as Tony touched her. She retrieved her car keys from her purse. "I've had a long day and drinking beer always makes me tired." She stood up and realized she had one too many beers. Her head felt a little dizzy, but cleared within a few minutes.

Tony stood up with her. "Are you okay? I think I should drive you home. I would like to spend more time with you," he whispered into her ear. "Maybe even see you again. If you leave now alone, that might never happen. Besides, I really care for your safety and I would not have you drive down the block. Please, let me drive you home. I don't want anything to happen to you."

Connie could not help noticing the resentment on Angie's face. The big-busted blonde made it clear she was out to get Tony, and gave Connie a look to let her know it. Tony had made his choice, and Connie accepted. "Okay, but I have to say good-bye to Loretta and Sam."

Tony gave her a warm smile and took her hand in his. "Let's go find them." They made their way back into the crowded apartment. The chatter of voices could be heard over the music. They soon spotted Loretta and Sam off in a nearby room. "Hey Sam," Tony said as they reached the couple. "Were going to take off. I wanted to wish you a happy birthday; I'll talk to you soon."

Connie saw the expression of shock come over Loretta's face. She knew instantly she would have to answer the who, what, and where questions. "I will call you tomorrow," she said to her friend.

As she started to walk away she felt a tug on her arm and knew Loretta was not going to wait until then to hear the story. She turned to Tony, "Will you wait for me outside? I will not be long," she reassured him. As soon as Tony was out of sight, Loretta grabbed Connie and led her to one of the bedrooms and closed the door behind them.

"What are you doing with Tony? Or maybe I should ask what are you going to do with Tony?" Loretta's voice reached a high-pitched whisper.

Connie did not want Sam to hear their conversation, although he probably knew why Loretta dragged her in there. "Loretta, calm down. Tony is just driving me home, that's all. I drank more than I am used to and he offered to take me home. It's as simple as that, no big deal," she emphasized.

Loretta eyed her friend suspiciously, "You seem fine to me. I can drive you home if you want. Look, I know Tony is good looking, but I have heard of his reputation with the women. And I do not think Rick would like this," she added.

"Rick's not here, is he?" Connie retorted. "And besides, how do you know Rick is the one for me? How will I know if I don't explore?"

"Oh, Connie," Loretta pleaded. "Don't be foolish; don't throw away what you have with Rick over some good looking guy that probably just wants a one night fling with you. Let me take you home," she urged.

"No," Connie yelled. "Look," she said, in a calmer voice, "I will call you tomorrow, I will be fine." She kissed her friend on the cheek. "Thanks for caring so much."

Loretta stood with her arms crossed staring down at the floor. "What good does it do? You don't listen to me." She then opened the door for Connie. "Just don't fuck him, okay?"

"I promise. I won't fuck him." Connie smiled at her friend. "You better get out there and join the party."

Connie said good-bye to Sam and found Tony outside waiting for her. "I am sorry about that," she said once they got into Tony's car. "I had to convince Loretta we weren't going to elope."

"Ah," Tony nodded as he started his car. "So that's what it was about. She doesn't approve of me, does she?" he teased. "That's okay, I've been under scrutiny before and I can handle it. Do you feel like getting a cup of coffee before I take you home?"

"That sounds good right now." Connie did not want the night to end just yet. She felt more awake since her little feud with Loretta. Tony shifted into gear and headed toward the nearest coffee shop. He talked more about his future in music and Connie thought it was fascinating. He wanted her to come hear them play and asked if she would come the following weekend. She did not know what to say. Rick would be back and they always spent the weekends together. Still she did not mention Rick's name, or her involvement with him. She did not know what to do. If she mentioned it, she might not see him again. Once seated in a booth, they ordered their drinks. Tony continued his discussion. Before Connie realized it, two hours had passed and the coffee shop was closing. "I'm really sorry; I didn't mean to keep you out this late." Tony apologized, "I have been enjoying your company so much, the time just flew." He took out his wallet and placed a five-dollar bill on the table.

She had still evaded the issue of seeing him next week. They left the restaurant and Connie gave directions to her house. They turned down her street and pulled into her driveway.

"This is your place?" He asked surprised. "This is a nice house." Tony looked through his windshield up at the two story colonial style brick house. "Even my parent's home is not this nice. And my dad makes a decent living. Do you live here alone?"

Connie laughed at his surprise. "Yeah, it's all mine. It was left to me when my parents died."

"I am sorry," Tony looked embarrassed. "I didn't mean to look like an idiot." I really would like to see you again." He watched as her expression changed. "What is it, Connie?" He urged, "Please tell me."

"Tony, I am involved with someone," she hesitated. "His name is Rick." She watched as his expression turned from concern to disappointment. "I'm sorry; I really should have mentioned it earlier. I was having such a good time with you I didn't want it to end."

"Well, I hope he knows how lucky he is to have you. If I

was not such a nice guy I might try to take you away from him," Tony teased. "There is something very special about you, Connie. I hope to see you again."

Connie was glad it was dark. She did not want him to see her blush. "It was nice meeting you, Tony," she said as she opened the car door. "Thank you for taking me home." He stayed in her driveway until she had her front door open. Then she turned and waved good-bye. Once she was inside, she realized her legs were trembling. What was it about Tony that excited her so much? Sure, he was good looking, but so was Rick. He had said she was special, or did he tell all the girls that? She wanted Tony to kiss her. Connie took off her shoes and walked into the living room, stopping to turn on a nearby lamp. She looked over at her answering machine to see the red light flashing. Rick must have called, she thought. She pressed the playback button. A few seconds later she heard his voice on the recorder. "Hi, it's me; I guess you ended up going to Sam's party. Just called to say I love you. I'll see you in a couple of days. Bye." Connie turned off the lamp and went upstairs to her room. Misty, who was lying on her bed, looked up and seemed to smile. Connie petted her until she could hear her purring. She undressed and climbed under the sheets. She imagined what it would be like to make love to Tony. Kissing him; feeling him against her; inside her. She could stand it no longer and with her hand she climaxed, wishing it was Tony doing these things to her body. Only then could she drift off to sleep. The next day, she showered, did her laundry and made an honest attempt to clean the house. She finished the kitchen, the living room and the two bathrooms. She was on her way to do her bedroom when Loretta rang the door. "If you're ready, I thought I could take you to get your car. It sure was some party last night? So what happened between you and Tony?"

"Well, we stopped and had coffee, stayed until the place closed. Then he took me home. And no, he didn't come in. And yes, I told him I was seeing someone. He was very disappointed." Connie did not want to elaborate on the subject.

"What did you think about him? Did he want to see you again?"

Connie realized her friend would not stop with the questions until she felt satisfied. "I think he is a really nice guy and very cute. And he did ask if I would come hear his band play this weekend.

"I'm sorry about last night, but Tony has a reputation of loving them and leaving them, if you know what I mean. The longest he has ever stayed with anyone, from what I heard, was four months.

Connie felt a twinge in her heart and tried not to let Loretta know it. "Let me go change clothes and then we can get my car." Connie hurried up the stairs and came back down after a few minutes. She grabbed her keys and locked the front door behind them. When they arrived in Sam's parking lot, Loretta pulled up to Connie's car. Connie thanked her friend and stepped out of the car. She turned and opened her car door and seemed surprised to find a dozen red roses lying on the car seat. "Loretta," she yelled, "Come here." Her friend was at her side immediately, alarmed by the sound of her voice. Connie retrieved the roses and smelled them. She then opened the note attached. "I hope these roses can persuade you to see me again. Love, Tony." Connie looked up at Loretta. "What should I do?"

"Oh, Connie, if you want my honest opinion I would say forget it. But knowing you, you are not going to listen, you're going to do what you want. He must have come over this morning after I left to find out which car was yours." Loretta looked around the parking lot to see if she could see his car. "I don't think he's in Sam's, do you want to come in?"

"No, I think I'll go home. Besides, if he were here I would not want him to see me with no make-up on. I look a mess. Thanks for the ride, I'll call you later." Connie gently laid the roses back on the car seat and climbed in behind the wheel. As she pulled away, she looked in her rear view mirror to see Loretta standing with her hands on her hips shaking her head. Connie stuck her arm out the window and waved. She felt as she was on cloud nine. She could hardly concentrate driving home. Monday and Tuesday came and went, and Connie was still in a dream state. She could not stop thinking about Tony.

Chapter eleven

Wednesday night Rick arrived home. He had been up since five that morning and felt exhausted. It was good to be home. His boss gave him the next two days off because of the business trip. He was looking forward to spending them with Connie. He thought about her the whole time. He could not wait to put his arms around her, to feel his body next to hers. He walked over to the phone and dialed her number. "Get ready," he said upon hearing her familiar voice. "I'll be by in half an hour and we'll get something to eat. He set the phone down and proceeded to throw some things into his overnight bag, and remembered the box of roses he had purchased for Connie at the airport. She will love these. He had never bought her roses before.

Connie hung up the phone and hurried around the house,

picking up the place. As she walked into the kitchen to put some dishes in the sink, her eyes came upon the vase that held the roses Tony had given her. She did not want to throw them away, but how could she explain them to Rick? She quickly grabbed a garbage bag from the closet and tossed them in. She then set the bag in the garage. She had just enough time to change clothes and apply fresh make-up. When she answered the door, Rick stood there holding red roses. The first thought that went through her head was he must have retrieved them from her garbage.

Rick laughed at her expression, "I know, I know, it's not like me to buy flowers. I wanted you to know how much I missed you." Rick took Connie into his arms and kissed her passionately.

Connie took the roses and set them in the same vase that held Tony's roses just a few minutes ago. She noticed Rick's overnight bag on the floor. "Oh, do you plan on spending the night?"

Rick smiled, "I have two days off. I thought we could make up for the lost weekend we missed." Rick grabbed her by the waist and gave her another kiss. "Let's stop off after dinner and grab a bottle of wine." Connie pulled away, and smiled wryly. She was a little irritated over the fact that he did not ask if it was okay with her. "Rick, I do have to work tomorrow."

He picked up the tension in her voice, "If you don't want me here just say so. This is not the way I expected you to react. I thought you would be elated with the idea of us being able to spend time together."

Connie realized Rick's feelings were hurt. "It's just that I wished you would have said something first, that's all. I haven't changed the sheets or stocked up on food." She was trying to make him feel better. "Come on, I am starving," she gave him a peck on the lips. They went to their favorite restaurant and afterward, Rick stopped and bought a bottle of wine. When they arrived back at Connie's, Rick started a fire while she lit some candles. They listened to their favorite radio channel that played slow love songs. Connie brought in two glasses and Rick poured the wine into them. They sat quietly in each other's arms watching the fire. Soon Rick started to kiss her. He took off her sweater and kissed her bare breasts. Connie moaned, and unzipped his pants and grasped his penis. His hands found her zipper and he gently pulled down her jeans and underwear. He then buried his hand into her warm spot. When her moans became louder, Rick quickly got on top and entered her. Afterward, they blew out the candles and went up to bed.

Chapter twelve

Rick woke up about nine o'clock and listened to the silence in the house. Connie must have left already, he thought. After taking a shower, he went downstairs and helped himself to a cup of coffee. He sat on the couch and turned on the TV. There was nothing on but talk shows, so he turned it off. He decided to have one more cup of coffee and then he would do some yard work. God knows, this place needs it, he thought. Connie barely kept up with cutting the grass. He went into the garage and started to look around for a pair of gloves he could wear. There was an old yellowish leather pair in a drawer by the tools. He then grabbed a pair of hedge clippers down from the rack. He opened the garage door and the light fell on the garbage pail. He saw something red and walked over to see what it was. "Roses, what the hell is this?" Rick saw there was a note attached and went to grab it along with some of the stems. He pricked his fingers on the thorns, but the pain he felt from them did not compare to the pain he felt in his heart as he read: "I hope these roses can convince you to see me again. Love, Tony."

Anger started to build up inside. Who the fuck was Tony? When was he with Connie? He threw the roses back into the garbage and stood there, staring at them. His mind was reeling. Connie was seeing someone else. The image of her in someone else's arms flashed through his mind. Rick kicked the garbage can, sending it flying into the driveway. The red roses spewed from the pail. He hands were clenched, wishing he could kick the shit out of this Tony character. That is why she made that remark about letting her know first, on spending the night. She probably had plans with him. That look she had when he showed up with roses. God, what a fool I am. He threw the gloves back on the table, closed the garage door, and went inside to grab his car keys. Once behind the wheel, he tried to think rationally. Maybe the roses were for someone else. No, why would they be in Connie's garbage? He drove into town and parked in front of the Local Press. As he entered, he saw Connie look up from the desk, smiling. "Who the fuck is Tony?" Rick screamed into her face. Connie's face showed confusion. "I found the roses he gave you."

Jim, her boss, entered the room. "Is there a problem, Connie?" he asked as his eyes turned to Rick.

"It's okay, Jim," she turned back to Rick and glared back at him. "We'll talk about this later."

"I want to talk about this now." He glared back. He did not want to give Connie time to think up an excuse.

Why don't you take an early lunch, Connie?" Jim suggested as a customer entered the store. "Go on," he insisted.

Connie came out from behind the counter and Rick followed her outside the store. They both got into his car where they could talk. "What the hell are you doing going through my garbage?"

"I was going to do some yard work around your house," Rick said sarcastically. "That's beside the point; who the fuck is Tony?"

"I didn't ask you to do any yard work around my house. And I don't want you going through my things."

"Your things?" Rick shouted back, "for Christ's sake, it was your garbage. You're avoiding my question. Are you fucking this guy, Connie?"

"No, I am not fucking this guy," she retorted. "Look, he's just someone I met at Sam's party and he gave me a ride home. And I do not think I owe you any explanation. How dare you come flying into where I work and start a scene. Do you know how much you just embarrassed me?"

Rick could not believe what he was hearing. "So you think I don't deserve an explanation? Well, I guess our relationship isn't what I thought it was. Good-bye Connie."

"Rick, I didn't mean that. I don't know what I meant. My emotions feel mixed up right now."

"Well, when you find out, let me know." Rick said very coldly. He knew she was crying, but he also felt hurt. Hurt by the fact she did not mention this Tony guy from the start. Hurt by the fact she did not think enough of their relationship to give him an explanation.

Connie wiped away her tears and got out of the car without a word. She watched as he drove off and waited a few minutes before going back into the store. She did not feel like working anymore today. She went to ask Jim if she could go home. She saw his concern when she wiped away her tears.

"I hope things work out for you, Connie," he said as she left.

"Thanks, Jim. I hope so too." There were not too many people in town that did not know she was Rick's girl, she thought. Sometimes someone would come into the store and remark on what a good-looking couple they made. "You seem so in love," Mrs. Evans would always say. Was she really in love with Rick? She knew from being in the newspaper business that looks could be deceiving. Things were not always the way they appeared to be.

Connie needed someone to talk to, so she drove to Loretta's. She knew her friend would be at work, but she had a key to her place. They had exchanged keys years ago, and this time it would come in handy. She would wait there for her friend to come home. Rick might be at her place and she did not want another confrontation. She was about to turn on the television when she saw Loretta's car pull in.

"I am surprised to see you here," Loretta said when she came through the door. "Oh, no! What happened? I can see you've been crying." Loretta laid down her purse on the nearby chair.

Fresh tears rolled down Connie's face, "It's Rick. We broke up. He found the roses Tony gave me and came to the Local Press and we had this huge fight." Connie grabbed a tissue from the blue and white box she had brought in from Loretta's bathroom. "I owe you a box of tissue," she said between tears.

"Oh, honey," Loretta went to sit down next to her friend on the couch. She put her arm around her. "Did you tell him there was nothing going on? I hate to see you this upset."

Connie nodded. "The whole thing just got out of hand. I said one thing and he said something else. He made me so mad coming into where I work like that and embarrassing me in front of Jim.

"Men can be such jerks, can't they? Give it a couple of days, I'm sure he'll call you and things will be the way they were." Loretta said, trying to reassure her friend.

"I don't know if I want things the way they were."

"I think this is you're first big fight with Rick and it will all blow over in a couple of days. Rick loves you, and you love him. You two were meant for each other. Any fool can see that. And I warned you that Tony was nothing but trouble. Now dry your tears and let me cook you some of my world famous spaghetti. And afterwards we'll go rent a movie, okay?"

Connie was not hungry, but agreed. An hour or so later, dinner was done. She had to admit, Loretta's spaghetti was too good to resist. They drove to the video store and finally agreed on a "Steven Segal" movie. It was late by the time the movie was over and Connie was ready to go home. She gave Loretta a hug. "Thanks for being here when I needed you."

"No problem," she hugged her back. "Call me tomorrow." She watched her friend get into the car, turned off the lights and went to bed.

Chapter thirteen

Connie had just finished vacuuming when she heard the phone ring. Since her fight with Rick, her heart would skip a beat every time it rang. It had been two weeks now and he had not called once. She missed him so much, and yearned to be in his arms again. Twice she had gone to call him, but lost her nerve. Maybe this time it was him. She held the receiver to her ear. "Hello," she said cautiously. "It's only me," Loretta said. "Look, do you want to stay home tonight and brood about Rick, or would you like to see Tony's band with Sam and me tonight? They're playing in town at the Pub, and Tony had asked Sam if you would come."

"I thought you didn't like the idea of me seeing Tony?" Connie remarked to her friend.

"Well, maybe you two are meant for each other, and who am I to interfere with destiny? Will you go or not?"

Connie looked at the clock on the mantle, she would have

to take a shower and eat. It was now going on six o'clock. If she did not go she would sit home alone thinking of Rick. "Okay, I'll go. What time should I be ready?"

"The band starts at nine; we'll pick you up at eight. That way we can find a good table to sit. You'll see, by the end of the night you will have forgotten all about Rick."

Connie laughed lightly, "I hardly think so. I'll see you at eight." She hung up the phone and hurried upstairs and turned on her shower. She quickly took off her clothes and stuck her hand under the water to test the temperature. Satisfied, she stepped into the tub.

Rick sat on his sofa staring at his TV, but thinking of Connie. He had missed her terribly and this whole thing was ridiculous. Last week, his company had sent him out of town again so it was not so bad. He had his work to keep him occupied. This weekend he was home, and all he could do was think about her. He could stand it no longer. He reached over and picked up the phone. He would tell her how much he loved her and say he was sorry. He just wanted his Connie back in his arms where she belonged. When he heard her voice on the answering machine, he hung up with disappointment.

Chapter fourteen

Connie was ready at eight sharp. She wore a yellow top neatly tucked into her light blue jeans. It showed off her thin figure. Her waist length silky dark hair enhanced her blue eyes. She heard Sam and Loretta pull up in the driveway. Connie locked up the house and ran to the car. It was a short trip to the pub and the parking lot seemed half filled. Once inside, they grabbed a table and a waitress appeared to ask them what they were drinking. Connie ordered a glass of wine and Loretta and Sam ordered a beer.

"I am glad you decided to join us," Sam told Connie. "I know Tony will be glad to see you," he said, looking around for him. "There he is," Sam waved his arm in the air. "Hey Tony. Over here." He spotted his friend fiddling with cable wires behind the stage.

Tony heard his name and looked up to see Sam, Loretta, and Connie. Seeing her again brought a smile to his face. He laid down the cables and strolled over to the table and sat down next to Connie. "I was worried you wouldn't come. Thanks for bringing her, Sam." He drew his attention back to Connie. She was so beautiful, he thought. It was the innocence that showed in her blue eyes that made him adore her. "I hope you like what we play tonight. We're trying out some new songs."

"Tony, we need you up on stage for a sound check," someone yelled from the stage.

"I have to go. I'll come back when we get a break." Tony stood up and walked over to the man holding a bass guitar. More people had come in and Loretta commented on how it was a good thing they came early. Shortly afterward, Tony went up to the mike and introduced the band. "Are you ready for some rock and roll?" Some people from the back yelled yeah, and the band broke into a fast beat song.

Connie seemed amazed on how good the band sounded. Especially Tony, he was so talented--and so good-looking. By the third song, people started to crowd the dance floor. Sam grabbed Loretta's arm and they disappeared into the crowd of bobbing heads. A cute looking guy approached Connie and asked if she wanted to dance. It had been years since she danced and did not feel confident. She thanked him politely and said no. He looked disappointed and went on to ask another girl at a nearby table. This time he was not rejected and Connie felt relieved. After a few more songs, Tony announced they were taking a break and would be back shortly. A few of the girls Connie recognized from Sam's party had gathered around back stage. She recognized Angie, who had given Connie a dirty look when

Tony left with her. This time she was hanging on the drummer. She kept rubbing her big tits against his arm. And by the expression on his face, he was enjoying it immensely. Tony soon joined her again at the table.

"So what did you think?" he asked, taking a sip from his glass of beer. "We're a little rusty because we haven't worked enough on the new material. But you can get a general idea on how we sound."

"I liked it a lot; your band is really good. And the people seem to like you as well." Connie said, noticing more people were coming through the door.

"We have a pretty good following. It helps to get gigs. Bars do not want to hire bands that do not draw a crowd 'cause then they lose money. The more people there are, the more alcohol they sell. Sam and Loretta came back to the table. Loretta had a fresh drink in her hand. "Wow, you guys are great." Her words slurred from the effects of the alcohol.

"You're just saying that 'cause your drunk," Tony teased. He turned his attention to Connie. "Can I buy you another one?" seeing her glass was almost empty.

"Yes, please," she smiled as she gazed into his blue eyes. Tony waived to the waitress and she came to the table and took his order. "This is the first time I've ever been here," Connie remarked as she looked around the place. "I must have driven past here a million times."

Tony looked surprised. "Where do you usually go on weekends? I know all the local bars in the area and this is probably the most decent."

Connie shrugged her shoulders, "I usually just stay home and watch television." She did not want to mention that it is usually over at Rick's that she does this.

"She lives a very sheltered life," Loretta commented.

"No, we've gone out to that place on Lake Street. It doesn't have bands, though."

"That's where I met you," Sam squeezed her leg under the table. "Have you been up there since?"

Loretta squeezed his leg back. "Now why would I go back there without you? I've found the man of my dreams." She picked up her glass, took a sip and winked at him. She then leaned over and kissed him tenderly on the lips.

Tony smiled as he shook his head and turned his attention back to Connie. "Will you wait for me after the show? I'll take you home."

Connie was hoping he would ask. "I guess I can," she smiled warmly.

"I have to get back up there again," Tony stood. "We have one more set to play and then I am yours," he grinned. Tony joined the other members on stage and spoke into the mike. "I would like to dedicate this next song to Connie." All eyes followed Tony's to the table where she sat. The guitar player started the slow ballad and as Tony began to sing, his attention was only on her. His voice flowed with background harmonies of the other band members.

Connie could not believe this was happening. She felt slightly embarrassed and thrilled that Tony was singing a beautiful love song to her. When the song ended, everyone applauded. The band then broke into an upbeat tempo and the dance floor filled once again with couples. Sam tried to get Loretta back up on the dance floor, but she had too much to drink and was afraid she would fall on her face. "Are you okay?" Connie asked, noticing Loretta did not look well.

"Yes, but I think we are going to leave soon. I need to get something to eat or I will be sick. You want to come with us? I heard Tony ask you to stay."

"You go ahead. I'll be okay. They probably have a few more songs and then they will be done. Connie knew by Loretta's expression that she felt concerned with leaving her alone. "I'll be fine. Don't worry."

"Are you sure it's okay?" Loretta stood up with Sam. "Call me tomorrow." Sam and Loretta waved to the band and then walked out the door.

The band finished after three more songs and Tony walked over to Connie. "I have to pack up so it'll be a few more minutes." The lights came on and the bartender called last call. Tony walked back to the stage and started to put his guitar in the case nearby.

Connie saw most of the people leaving and saw Angie hanging around the stage, waiting for the drummer, she presumed. A waitress went around to the empty tables picking up glasses and emptying ashtrays.

"I suppose you are waiting for someone in the band?" The waitress with the long blonde hair and tight jeans asked.

"Yes, I am," Connie replied. She wanted to add, "What business is it of yours?" but did not. After a short time,

Tony grabbed his coat and walked over to Connie.

"Everyone is going over to the drummer's house. Do you want to go? If not, that's okay. We can do something else." Tony put on his black leather jacket that looked so good on him.

"Well, maybe for a little bit." Connie could not think of any place to go and she did not want to give Tony the wrong impression if they went back to her house. She stood up and put on her jacket.

Tony smiled, "Let's go." They went out to the parking lot where some of the band members were waiting. "We will meet you there," he called to the others. He took out his keys and unlocked Connie's door and opened it for her. He then got in on the driver's side. Soon as the car started, music blared from the radio. Tony quickly lowered the volume. "Sorry about that. I always forget to turn it down." He put it in drive and they headed out of the parking lot.

As they pulled out, Connie looked over at the group that was standing by a van. She recognized Angie and the waitress who had asked if she was waiting for someone in the band. She was glad she did not say anything snotty to her. The group piled into the van and proceeded to follow Tony and Connie. Soon they were on a country road and Connie noticed how clear the stars stood out in the sky. Tony turned down a dirt road that seemed to go on forever. Finally, they came to an old two-story farmhouse that needed repair.

"This is Ted's the drummer's house. We practice here and it's great. No one can hear us so no one can complain."

Connie and Tony got out of the car and waited for Ted to arrive. When everyone got out of the van, they followed Ted into the house. Immediately, a dog started to bark and came to the door, sniffing and waging his tail.

"Down, boy," the drummer yelled as he switched on a light so everyone could see their way in. They all gathered into the living room, which was large. Ted went into the kitchen toward the back door to let his dog outside. On his way back he opened the refrigerator and took out a twelve pack of beer to pass around. There was always beer in the house. If he did not buy it, someone would bring it in and leave it there. He returned to the living room, sat in his favorite chair, and after taking a beer for himself, passed it around. Angie quickly sat on the floor next to him. It was obvious she was very drunk and Ted knew he would be having a good time with her later. Most of the time, he knew Angie wanted Tony. But tonight, Tony brought someone with him. Someone he had never met before. The new chick was beautiful, Ted thought to himself. Those blues eyes of hers were hypnotizing. He gazed at her figure and felt himself becoming excited. Maybe Tony would share her as he did the others. He did not mind Tony's leftovers.

Connie was sitting next to Tony on the couch and took a beer from his hand when he offered it to her. She felt very uncomfortable but tried not to show it. Tony must have sensed this she thought, because he then put his arm around her. She looked around the room and noticed it was very neat. The furniture was cream colored and matched everything else. On one side of the room there was a large fireplace. Connie thought the house had to have been built in the eighteen hundreds. The blonde waitress from the bar turned to Connie and introduced herself as Sherry. They started up a conversation. They talked about where Sherry worked, and Connie talked about her job. Tony seemed engrossed in another conversation with his bass player about their next gig. The beer made Connie relax a little but when Tony asked if she wanted another one, she refused.

Tony watched as Ted and Angie went upstairs and he looked at his watch that gave the time of three-thirty. "Connie, I think we should go. It's getting late and I'm really beat."

"Sure," she said, putting the can down on the coffee table. "Well, it was nice meeting you, Sherry."

"It was nice meeting you, too," she smiled. "Tony, you have to bring her around more often."

Tony smiled at Sherry. "I will. See you later. Good-bye, everyone." Connie stood up and followed Tony out the door.

Once outside, Tony gently grabbed Connie's arm, turned her towards him and pulled her into his arms. He then brushed away a strand of hair from her face and kissed her soft lips. "I have wanted to do this all night," he whispered into her ear. Tony felt a nudge between his legs and looked down to see Ted's retriever waging his tail. "Did Ted forget you, boy?" Tony teased. "I'd better get him inside." Tony left Connie's arms but returned a minute later. "Now, where were we?" he asked as he took her into his arms again and kissed her. "I'd better take you home before I forget what a nice guy I am." He walked around to the passenger's side and opened the door for Connie.

Connie felt relieved that Tony did not expect anything from her tonight. Even though she longed to give herself to him, it was too soon. His respect for her made her want him even more.

Tony pulled into Connie's driveway and shifted into park. "Can I call you?"

Connie took out a pen and a scrap of paper and jotted down her number. "I'm usually home by five during the week."

Tony leaned over and kissed her again. "I'll call you tomorrow."

Chapter fifteen

He waited until she was safely inside before driving home. He could not wait until he saw her again. He felt like the luckiest guy in the world. Now he was curious about the other guy. He remembered she had mentioned a boyfriend before, but Sam told him they were no longer seeing each other. He did not want to hear anything different from her so he did not ask. She was with him tonight, which is all that mattered. He wondered who broke up with whom, what was he like. Was this guy going to come after him for seeing Connie? He was not too worried about that. He could take care of himself. He was in good shape, being in construction and moving heavy band equipment kept him that way. He had been in a serious fight two years ago. Some jealous boyfriend showed up at a job site and accused Tony of sleeping with her. He knew the girl but he never had sex with her. The guy was drunk and would not listen to anyone. He took a swing at Tony, but missed. The second time he swung, Tony blocked his arm and punched the shit out of him, knocking the poor bastard to the ground. Tony thought that was the end of it and started back on stage. When the guy stood up, he went over to his girlfriend and started wailing on her. The girl's mouth was bleeding pretty badly. Tony grabbed the guy and yelled. "You think your tough hitting a woman? Well come on asshole let's see what you got." He dragged the jerk outside and Tony ended up breaking his nose. Someone called the police and everyone at the bar said the other guy started it. The police arrested him after seeing his girlfriend's face. Someone later took her to the hospital where she needed a couple of stitches. Tony never saw the girl around after that, and he was glad. The band did not need troublemakers following them around and giving them a bad reputation. Tony's thoughts returned to Connie. He was glad she went with him to Ted's. If she had said no he probably would have taken Angie home and fucked her all night long as he did so many other nights. Angie was one of the many girls that wanted him. Getting laid was not his primary goal this evening. Getting to know Connie was. He found her to be beautiful, and her slender body excited him. He was eager to learn more about her, which surprised him. Most women he dated did not interest him very much. They all wanted to please him anyway they could and after awhile the relationship would get boring. Tony would go looking for someone new, leaving behind someone's heart he had broken. For him, it was the same thing over and over. This time something was different, he was sure of it.

Chapter sixteen

Connie looked at herself in the full-length mirror. She had been shopping most of the day trying to find new clothes to wear. She had purchased a couple of new style jeans everyone seemed to be wearing and a black leather vest. She just finished applying her make-up when the doorbell rang. Connie quickly ran down the stairs, knowing it was Tony. This would be the fourth time he had come over to her house. She still had not invited him to spend the night and wondered if he was getting anxious. She did not know how much longer she could contain her own desires. She wanted to know him better before sleeping with him. She could never just hop into bed with a man. It was not her style.

"Wow, you look great." Tony took her into his arms and kissed her. "I'll have to keep an eye on you tonight and make sure no one tries to steal you away from me." Tony followed her in and sat on the couch while she finished getting ready. Tony looked at the clock on the mantle. "Babe, come on," he yelled. "I told the guys we'd be there at seven." The phone on the end table started to ring.

Connie yelled from another room. "Can you answer that please?"

On the second ring, he said, "Hello." There was silence on the other end. "Is there someone there," he asked. Still silence. Then a man's voice spoke. "Sorry, I must have dialed wrong." The line went dead. Tony hung up the phone.

Connie was trying to get an earring in when she walked into the living room to see who was on the phone. "Who was it?"

"Some guy said he had the wrong number." Tony hesitated, "Connie, are you still seeing that guy?"

"No," Connie insisted. "It probably was the wrong number." She wondered if it was Rick, what he would think if he heard a guy answer. Would he try to call back? Tony stood up seeing Connie was ready to go. "I have no reason to doubt you," he said as he turned to face her. "And if you are seeing someone else, that would be okay. I mean…" he hesitated, "I don't know where I'll be in a year from now; I'm hoping the guys and I will get a contract. And there is a really good chance of that happening. We're almost done with making that demo we've been working on and then were sending it out to recording companies."

Connie smiled. "Fine, I hope you do get signed. I think that would be great. Can we go now?"

Tony kissed her gently on the lips and then followed her

out the door. They arrived at the bar the same time as the other band members. Connie spotted Sherry and joined her at the table.

"You're not working tonight?" Connie asked, remembering their conversation at Ted's. Sherry worked just about every weekend.

Connie was glad she would not be sitting by herself while the band played. The last gig she and Tony went to, every guy in the place was after her because she sat alone.

"I was able to switch nights with another waitress. Last time the band played out I had to work. Did I miss any thing? Tony said he brought you with him that night."

"The guys were great, but the place was a dump. When did Tony tell you that?"

"He was over at Ted's the other night." Sherry looked around the room and then lowered her voice. "I think Tony has it real bad for you," she said smiling. "You're all he can talk about. Even the other guys have said you've got him hooked. It was so funny seeing Angie get so pissed off when Tony brought you to Ted's. God, where are the waitresses around here?" Sherry stood up pulling money from her pocket. "I'm going to the bar. What do you want?"

Connie quickly gave Sherry a five, "glass of red wine, thanks." She watched Sherry walk to the bar and wondered what Tony was saying that made Sherry think he had it bad for her. She turned her attention to Tony on the stage. He was so good looking. She then thought of Rick and wondered if that was him that called. She still could not believe it was finished. What would she do if he wanted her back? She was starting to care very deeply for Tony but there was no way she was about to let him in on that. Not yet, it was too soon. Especially after his little speech about not knowing where he would be in a year from now. Tony came by the table to sit before the band had to play. Sherry returned with the drinks and complained about the lousy service. "Are Loretta and Sam coming?" Tony asked Connie.

"I don't think so; she said something about just staying in tonight." Connie felt the coolness of her drink that she held between her hands. She picked up the glass and slowly brought it to her lips. The summer nights were becoming increasingly warm and the cold refreshing glass of wine tasted so good. The ceiling fans gave some relief but not much. "It's so warm in here," she commented, as she took off her leather vest.

"Yes, I'd better see if they can turn on some air, or it's going to be one miserable night on stage under those hot lights." Tony walked over to the doorman and explained the situation.

"I am sorry bud," the big burly man said to Tony. "The air conditioning in this place has been out for a week now. I can leave the door open but that's the best I can do."

Tony thanked the guy and went back to Connie. "He just told me the air is out. At least Ted has his fan. I have to tell the guys. I'll be back."

Connie watched as Tony confronted the rest of the band about the problem. No one looked happy, she thought. Tony then went to the bar and bought himself a drink and a glass of red wine and came back to the table. "Drink up, Connie; it's going to be a long night."

"This place is a dump. No waitresses, no air conditioning. If the band plays this joint again, I'm not coming." Sherry said to Tony.

"I would not blame you," Tony agreed. "If they want us back they're going to have to pay some decent money." He took a sip from his drink and said, "It's time to start." He kissed Connie and went on stage. The rest of the guys stood ready to play. Tony grabbed the mike, "Hi, there. I know it's hot but just sit back and drink whatever suits you and enjoy the music." The guitar player broke into the lead guitar and Tony's voice followed. By the fourth song, Tony asked if they could turn down the stage lights. They did, and someone off stage yelled if that was better. "Yeah, thanks man," Tony said into the mike. "Now this next song is for a very special lady in the audience." He turned his attention towards Connie and began to sing.

"See what I mean," Sherry whispered into Connie's ear. "He's never dedicated songs to anyone. Has he done this before?

Connie nodded remembering how embarrassed she was the first time he sang to her. She felt more comfortable about it now. It was as if he was telling everyone in the room she belonged to him.

Sherry smiled. "You have to admit, it's probably the most romantic thing a guy could do, besides sending roses or declaring his love for you by hiring a sky writer."

The song ended and Connie told Sherry how she went to

get her car the next day from Sam's and found the dozen red roses in her car.

"No shit?" Sherry squealed, feeling the effects of the beer. "Do you know every girl in Kane County has tried to get him?" Sherry laughed and slapped her hand down on the table. "Well either you haven't slept with him yet or you have money."

The way Sherry said it made Connie burst out laughing. She was on her third glass of wine and feeling no pain. "Both," she said loudly. Seeing Sherry's eyes widen in shock made Connie laugh more.

"No shit?" Sherry started laughing, "I am sorry. I did not mean anything by it."

"That's okay," Connie said smiling. How long have you known Tony?

"About two years, maybe longer. I knew him before he started playing with these guys. He would come in the place I use to work every Friday night. Anyway, we became friends.

Tony announced they would be back after a fifteen-minute break. He jumped down from the stage and joined Connie and Sherry at the table. "What were you two laughing about?" He sipped from his glass and sat back in his chair. Connie thought about telling him but decided against it. "When?" She asked, acting as if she did not know what he meant.

"Never mind," Tony said. "I want this evening to end quickly. The whole band feels the same way. It's miserable on stage. Even though they turned down the stage lights it is still hot as hell." He looked at his watch. "Just one more hour."

"You look tired." Connie took her hand and placed it on his thigh.

Tony felt Connie's hand on his leg. He leaned over and kissed her.

"Come on, you two," Sherry said, becoming annoyed. "Don't you know how rude it is to kiss in front of other people?"

"I am sorry, Sherry," Connie said. "We'll try and behave ourselves."

"That's okay; I think I'm going to head for home. It's getting late and it's too warm in here. I'll see you two later." Sherry stood up and took her car keys from her purse and smiled. She bent down to Connie and whispered, "Don't make him suffer too much longer." Connie smiled back, acknowledging their earlier conversation.

"I got to go back on stage." Tony said after looking at his watch. "One more hour and we can leave this dump." Tony looked into Connie's beautiful face and kissed her.

There were fewer people on the dance floor. Connie went to the bar and bought herself another glass of wine. The band finished their last set and when the crowd yelled for an encore, Tony apologized and started to pack up the equipment. They were soon finished and he joined Connie outside. The cool air was refreshing.

"We were invited to go to Ted's. Do you want to go?" Tony said as they headed towards the car.

"Why don't we go back to my house?" Connie did not want to go to Ted's, not tonight. She had planned tonight to be special. She wanted Tony, and could not deny her feelings anymore. Once they arrived, Connie fixed Tony a cool glass of wine. She did not have any beer in the house and he said wine would be fine.

Connie knew Tony was watching her as she stood at the counter and poured the red wine into the glasses filled with ice. She turned to face him and held out the glass. Tony came to her, took the wine from her delicate hand and took a sip. He then placed the glass on the counter and took her into his arms and kissed her passionately. Connie leaned into him, letting him know she wanted him. He took off her shirt and undid her bra, letting her clothes fall to the floor. He reached for her firm breasts and gently caressed them until she moaned with excitement. She took his hand and led him upstairs to her room. He pulled off his shirt and undid her jeans as she leaned against the wall. He slipped his hand down to her soft hairs. Pulling down her jeans, and then her panties, he began to kiss her warm mound. Her legs began to tremble, and he quickly removed the rest of his clothing. He started to lead her to the bed when she whispered hoarsely. "No . . . here . . . now." She felt him enter her and she quickly climaxed.

Chapter seventeen

Time passed slowly since Rick had that terrible fight with Connie. He started going to another restaurant because the other one held to many memories for him. He worked longer hours then he had to hoping to get his mind off Connie. By the time he came home he felt exhausted. She was in his heart no matter where he went or what he did. His friends at work knew what was going on in his personal life. They tried to set him up with girls that they knew, but he was not interested. Connie was his first true love, and nobody could ever change that.

Rick sat in his car outside Connie's house waiting for her friend to leave. He had decided to come over and talk to her when he saw the car pull in her driveway. He thought she would go in alone. Instead he watched as a tall blonde guy followed her inside. Rick's emotions began to sink, realizing Connie's friend was not leaving. He started his car and slowly pulled away.

Chapter eighteen

Connie felt like a new person. Even Loretta had noticed it. She did not feel so sweet and innocent as she did with Rick. Being with Tony made her feel wild. She enjoyed going to the gigs with him and he would always sing that special song to her. She had become good friends with Sherry and sensed Loretta was jealous. She would make coy remarks about Sherry whenever Connie brought up her name. Tony's band had finished their demo and was in the process of sending the tapes out to recording studios. Connie thought about Rick often and wondered if he was seeing anyone. At times she wished she could see him but knew it would only complicate matters. Things were so different with Tony, even the sex. He always made her come. With Rick, she pretended she did. There were things she felt with Rick that she did not feel with Tony. Security was one; she knew where her relationship was with Rick. He always told her that he loved her and would ask, "Are you still my girl?" Remembering the way he use to say that brought tears to her eyes and made her heart ache for him. Tony kept his feelings to himself. Even after four months of seeing each other, never once did he indicate how he felt about her. They were together every weekend regardless whether the band played or not. He called every other night. Sherry had told her it was the longest relationship she ever remembered Tony having. Ted had even mentioned to her one evening after a gig that Tony had special feelings for her. Everyone seemed to know this but her.

Connie walked into the bakery as she did every Friday morning for her long johns. Mrs. Evans talked about the weather and filled her in on the latest gossip.

"What do you think about old Peterson's shack burning down?" Mrs. Evans squinted her eyes, revealing she knew more than what was printed in the paper. "I strongly suspect two teenagers that are trouble makers in town. I heard they were seen going into the police station with the sheriff later that same day."

The bell above the door rang as another customer entered the bakery. Connie did not wish to contribute to the rumor spreading and took the white paper bag from Mrs. Evans. "Have a nice day," she smiled as she headed outside. She then went to work. An hour later, Jim gave Connie an article to proofread. It stated the sheriff had hired the two boys Mrs. Evans had mentioned to go door to door and conduct a survey on recycling bins. Connie shook her head in dismay. Thanks to Mrs. Evans the two boys will probably get doors slammed in their faces, she thought.

Connie had been staring out the window when she spotted Rick's car pull up across the street. Her heart began to pound. She watched as he approached the Local Press and entered.

"Hello Connie," Rick said coldly as he stood across from her. "I'm here to place an ad."

"Hello, Rick," Connie tried to keep her hands from trembling as she grabbed a form. "What kind of ad do you want to place?" It was a question she had to ask everyone. She looked up from the sheet and noticed he looked as handsome as ever. His soft brown eyes that would twinkle when he smiled at her and his lips she would never kiss again.

I'm going to be moving and I'm hoping to sell all my furniture. Living room set, dining set, bedroom set."

Connie felt taken by surprise. "You're moving? Where?" She knew how much Rick loved the area. He had grown up here like she did. His family lived here, so did his friends.

"The company is opening a branch down south and has offered me a promotion to help get things started."

Connie's heart sank with disappointment. "I'm happy for you, Rick. If that is what you really want. I wish you the best of luck." What else could she say, Rick please do not go? It was too late for that. She swallowed the lump that was forming in her throat and looked down on the form. "What would you like the ad to say?"

"How about, Moving sale, everything must go. Best

offer. And then my address. That should do it. I hope to get rid of everything by the end of the month."

She read the ad back to him and gave him a price. He wrote out a check and handed it to her. Her hands trembled a little as she accepted it. "Will you call me before you go?" She didn't care if she was making a fool out of herself. She might never see him again. "Maybe we can have dinner or something." "Okay," Rick seemed surprised. "How about I call you next Sunday?"

Connie agreed. "Next Sunday will be fine." She watched as Rick left the store. She new Jim had been watching from the back room. Probably to make sure there was no trouble like the last time Rick was here. As she stood staring at the form for the ad, a tear slipped down her cheek falling on to the paper, leaving a wet blotch on the word 'moving'.

Rick sat in his car, his heart racing. It had been very difficult seeing her again. What he did not tell her was that he had asked for the job. He could not stay in town any longer. It brought to many painful memories for him. Everywhere he went he was reminded of Connie. The restaurants, the movie theater, and the roads he traveled on every day. He had thought long and hard about the move and felt this was the best thing he could do. He knew she was still seeing that guy. He almost ran into them twice, once at a restaurant and another time at the mall. He needed to get on with his life, and he could not do that living so close to her. Could he be mistaken, or did her eyes seem to get misty when he told her he was moving?

Chapter nineteen

"Hi, Tony," Connie tried to catch her breath. She had been out in the garage cleaning when she heard the phone ring and hurried in to answer it.

"Babe, can you be ready early? I need extra time setting up for tonight's gig." Tony's voice grew with excitement. A man by the name of Mike O'Day from Tri Recording Company was coming to hear the band play tonight. They sent him a tape and he responded three weeks later. He made it perfectly clear, he was just coming to hear them play, nothing more. "Just think, Connie. If this Mike O'Day likes us, it could mean a contract. We've put in extra practice time at Ted's today and we're going to sound great. At least the lounge we'll be playing tonight is decent. So, what do you think?"

"Tony, I'm sure this Mike O'Day guy is going to like what he hears." Feeling Tony's excitement, Connie giggled. "If you want me to be ready early, I'd better get started."

Two hours later he was at her door. "You look especially beautiful tonight," he said as he kissed her gently on the lips. "I'm glad to have you by my side on one of the most important nights of my life. I'm a nervous wreck. Does it show?"

Connie laughed. "No one will know. For the last two weeks all anyone could talk about was this Mike O'Day coming to hear them play. Let's go," she said, grabbing her purse.

They showed up at the lounge and most of the other guys were already there. Connie sat at a table that would seat Sherry, Loretta, and Sam. The place was nearly packed when Sherry came in. A couple of times people asked Connie if the two empty chairs next to her were taken.

"Have you seen him yet?" Sherry was referring to Mike O'Day. A waitress came to the table and took their order. "No," said Connie. "I'll have a glass of red wine," she told the waitress. "Look," she said, noticing a tall guy she did not recognize talking to Tony and Ted. "I bet that's him." They watched as the three men stood talking about something. Tony threw his head back and started laughing. Apparently something the stranger had said. The soundman now joined them but it seemed he was just letting them know it was almost time to start. The stranger shook hands with Tony and Ted and took a seat at a nearby table that had a reserved card.

Loretta and Sam came in and looked around the lounge until they spotted Connie. Loretta looked disappointed to see Sherry at the table. They walked over and sat down.

"I am glad you came," Connie said to her friend. She wanted to tell her about Rick coming into the Local Press. It would have to wait. She did not want to say anything in front of Sherry.

"We wouldn't miss tonight for anything." Loretta assured Connie. "When they become big at least Sam and I can say we knew them before they were rich and famous."

"Yeah, right," Sam remarked. "I think everyone is making way too much out of this guy Mike O'Day. He probably listens to four or five bands a week. And I'm sure he doesn't sign them all."

Connie did not like what he said but she had to agree. Maybe they were making too much of a thing about tonight. Maybe they were setting themselves up for disappointment. The band was ready and they broke into their opening song. The first set went really well. By the second set, the dance floor was crowded. A waitress came to the table and Sam was buying the next round. "What are you drinking, Connie?" Sam asked, giving the waitress his empty glass.

"I think I'll pass. Thanks anyway. My stomach's been upset lately. It's probably something going around." There were not too many times in Connie's life that she was sick. Every third year she came down with a head cold. And about every fourth year she came down with the flu. She tried to take a sip of her wine. It was no use it just turned her stomach. Instead, she asked the waitress for a glass of ice water. The band started to play a song that seemed to be everyone's favorite. Sam grabbed Connie by the arm and got her on the dance floor. She started to dance to the beat and suddenly the room began to spin. She stopped dancing and tried focusing her eyes on Sam. The last thing she remembered before losing consciousness was Sam's expression.

Tony watched as Connie's complexion turned white as she passed out cold into Sam's arms. He suddenly stopped playing, much to the dismay of the other band members. Tony set down his guitar and ran to Connie's side. She was still out cold. Loretta and Sherry were also there. The manager came over to see what the problem was. "She's probably had too much to drink, he said. Why don't you have one of her friends take her home?"

"She's not drunk; she only drank half a glass of wine," Loretta said sarcastically.

"Hey, Tony, are you going to play or not?" Ted yelled from the stage. "It figures, Ted said to the bass player. The one important night of our lives and this chick is going to blow it for us."

The bass player came over to Tony. "Look, Ted's right. Get this taken care of fast and get back on stage."

Connie came to and noticed everyone around her. "What happened?"

"You passed out cold, right into my arms." Sam said. "Are you okay? You don't look too good."

"Why don't you have Loretta and Sam take you home? I am sorry babe, but I have to stay here. I'll call you soon as we're done." He seemed concerned about Connie and kissed her lightly on the lips.

"Okay," she agreed and stood up on her own. "I'm sorry Tony, I don't know what happened." She felt embarrassed about causing such a commotion. "I feel fine now, but I think I'll go home." She kissed Tony good-bye, and said good-bye to Sherry.

"Call me." Sherry said, shaking her finger at her. She watched as the three of them walked out the door. Everyone went back to their seats.

Tony went back on stage. "Okay, folks," Tony spoke into the mike. "I'm sorry for the delay, but we're back now. This next one is for the special lady that isn't feeling well."

Before getting into Sam's car, Loretta whispered, "I think it would be a good idea if I talk to Connie alone. Can we drop you off first and then I'll take Connie home? I'll come over later." Loretta asked very sweetly.

Sam hesitated, "Well you did drink a couple of beers but I know you're okay to drive." On the way to Sam's apartment it was quiet in the car. Loretta sat up front and Connie sat in the back. "I hope you feel better, Connie," he said before getting out of the car. He kissed Loretta good-bye. "Please drive carefully."

"Look, I am fine," Connie insisted once they were alone. "You're making too big of a thing out of this. I didn't eat dinner because Tony was in such a hurry to get to the bar. Drinking on an empty stomach can do that, you know." "You drank a half of glass of wine." Loretta pulled into an all night pharmacy. "Wait here. I'll be right back." Loretta turned off the car and ran into the store. She quickly returned in five minutes.

"What did you get? I hope it's edible." Connie grabbed the bag that was sitting between her an Loretta and opened it. "Why the hell did you buy this?" Connie said pulling out the home pregnancy test.   "Oh my God, you do not think . . . I could not be . . ." Connie's mind began to whirl. When she got home she would look on her calendar to see when her last period was. "I can't be pregnant, I take the pill." Connie knew she had missed taking them two days in a row. Loretta pulled into Connie's driveway and both girls hurried into the house. Connie went around and turned on the lights. She ran upstairs to look on her calendar that she pinned on her wall next to her dresser. She counted the days since her last period. She felt a little better. She was only three days late, nothing new for her. She joined Loretta in the living room. "So, what do I have to do?"

Loretta handed her the box. "Pee on the stick and then we wait to see what color it turns."

Connie took the box and sat down next to her friend. "What if I am? I wanted to tell you earlier but Sherry was sitting with us. I saw Rick. He's moving down south."

"We can talk about that later. Go pee," Loretta urged. She watched as Connie went into the washroom. Loretta sat back on the couch and turned on the TV with the remote. She flipped through the channels, not really watching.

Connie came out of the washroom crying. Her face was whiter than when she fainted. "I'm pregnant. What am I going to do?" She had never anticipated getting pregnant. She had been taking the pill since she started seeing Rick. That was three years ago.

Loretta's eyes showed deep compassion as she went over to Connie and gave her a hug. "It'll be okay," she consoled her friend. "Things will work out. You'll see. You have options and you need time to think about them. Talk it over with Tony and see what he thinks."

Connie nodded her head and wiped away her tears. She was grateful for Loretta being with her at a time like this. Just like the night her parents died.

Chapter twenty

It was two o'clock in the morning when the band finished their last set. The guys started to pack up when Mike O'Day walked up to them. "I really like your sound and I think we can do business together. Here's my card. Give me a call in a couple of days and we will set up an appointment for you to come in and talk. You guys don't have an agent or a lawyer, right?"

Tony looked at the other guys in the band and then back at Mike O'Day. "No, we don't. Do we need one?"

"Yes you will need someone to look over the contracts before you sign them. We can recommend a few agencies that have worked with various bands. But the decision has to be yours. Whoever you decide to hire will be working very closely with you. It's important that everyone gets along. We don't want to sign a contract with you and then have problems in the band. We can talk more when you come into my office. I'll send you a list of agents you can call, and don't wait around to choose one. We want to start things rolling as soon as possible." He shook hands with the band members. "Call me in a couple of days."

"Alright!" Ted yelled when Mike O'Day was out the door. "Man, do you believe this? We're going to be signing a contract with one of the largest recording companies. Man, is this great or what? Hey girls, come here. We're definitely going to celebrate tonight." Sherry and Angie came over quickly to join them. They were standing in the background watching the guys talk to Mike O'Day.

The owner of the lounge was standing behind the bar and overheard. "Hey, come over here and make a toast," he said opening a bottle of champagne. He then grabbed some wine glasses from behind the counter. "I want you guys to send me an autographed picture when you are done with your recording. I'll put it right over there." He pointed to wall by the front door. And remember, this is the place where it happened."

Mike O'Day drove to the nearby hotel where he was staying. He felt pleased with the band. And having a good looking lead singer like Tony was an added bonus. Girls will go nuts over him. Mike O'Day smiled and shook his head. What a lucky guy. He will get conceited like the rest of them. Knowing you can have any girl in the world can do strange things to your head.

Tony drank the last of the champagne from his glass. "I should call Connie and see how she is."

"Man, it's almost three, she's probably asleep. You can call her tomorrow," Ted said. "Let's go back to my place and finish celebrating." He grabbed Angie around the waist and kissed her playfully on her neck. "Are you ready, baby?"

Chapter twenty one

Connie felt exhausted and her emotions were a wreck. She was unable to sleep after Loretta left. She kept thinking of how she was going to break the news to Tony. She had dozed off for an hour on the couch, waiting to hear from him. He never called or came over to her house. It was now noon and she decided to go lay down when the phone rang. She quickly picked up the receiver.

"Hi, do you still want to go out for dinner?" Rick asked hearing Connie's voice.

"Oh Rick," Connie said, remembering this was the Sunday they were to have dinner. "I'm not really feeling well. Can we make it another night?"

His voice sank with disappointment. "I've been looking forward to seeing you. I only have two more weeks before I move. What's wrong, Connie? You don't sound well. Is it the flu?"

It was a good thing Rick could not see her face. She

looked very sullen and withdrawn. Tears from the previous night had streaked her flawless complexion with black mascara. "It must be the flu," she stated, trying to hide her emotions over the phone. "Can you call me in a couple of days? Maybe I'll feel better then."

"Sure, Connie," Rick said sensing something was terribly wrong. "I hope you feel better."

Rick hung up the phone and thought about driving over to her place. She had not left his mind for a second since he saw her last. On second thought, he decided he would call back in a couple of days. He looked around his apartment and most of his furniture had been sold. There were boxes everywhere. He sat on one of the remaining chairs, staring at the contents in one of the boxes. Even if there was a chance of getting back with Connie, he still had made the commitment of taking the job down south.

Chapter twenty-two

It was nearly four-thirty when Connie woke from her nap. She went down stairs to check her answering machine. No one had called. She made herself a small pot of coffee to help her wake up. After taking a shower she felt a lot better. At six-thirty she decided to call Tony. There was no answer. At eight-thirty, the doorbell rang. She looked out the side window next to her door and saw Tony. She unlocked the door and he came in and kissed her.

"I'm sorry I didn't call. It was so late by the time we got through and I figured you would be asleep."

Connie could smell the alcohol from the previous night still on Tony's breath. "I called your place two hours ago." Connie walked into her living room and sat on the sofa. Tony sat next to her.

"I haven't gone home yet. I spent the night at Ted's. Connie, I am still reeling from the excitement. Mike O'Day wants us to sign a contract. Can you believe it?"

"That's great," Connie said, surprised. She had forgotten all about Mike O'Day.

"He wants us to find an agent, one that we can get along with. We're to call him in a few days to set up an appointment. This is my dream come true. Connie you don't know how bad I wanted this." Tony yawned, "I am beat. We stayed up all last night celebrating."

The last statement irritated Connie. "I was up all last night, too. You should have called, Tony. You haven't asked me once how I am. You've been going on and on about the band. Did you forget last night I passed out on the dance floor?"

Tony rubbed his forehead, "I just figured you had too much to drink. Don't start bitching. I'm too tired right now. Are you okay?"

"No I am not okay," Connie started to cry.   "I'm pregnant." This was not the way she wanted to tell him.

"You're pregnant?" Tony raised his voice as he stood up and started to walk around the room. "This is not a good time, Connie. I mean, I'm going to be on the road. I won't be around to be a daddy. I'm not ready for that."

"I didn't plan this, Tony." Connie was getting angry with him. "It's not something I'm ready for, either. I don't know what to do."

"Are you sure? Maybe your wrong."

"I'm not wrong. Loretta stopped off on the way home last night and picked up a pregnancy test. And I haven't been feeling well."

Tony sat down and put his head between his hands,

looking down at floor. "I think an abortion is the only way to go. Connie I'm not going to lie to you. I'm not ready to settle down and raise a family. I might never be."

"An abortion?" Connie was shocked. She did not know of anyone that had one. She guessed they were common. Still, the thought scared her.

"I'll go with you and of course I'll pay for it. But it has to be done soon, before I go on the road." He put his arm around her. "It'll be okay, I promise."

Connie felt scared inside and having Tony's arm around her didn't make her feel any better. She realized after all these months Tony never once said he loved her. As for her own feelings, she thought she was in love with him. Now, she was not sure.

"Connie, I have to get home and get some sleep." Tony stood up to leave. "I can't think right now. I'll call you tomorrow and we'll talk more about this."

Connie walked him to the door and he kissed her goodnight. She felt deeply depressed after he left. She called Loretta and cried over the phone. "He wants me to have an abortion."

Loretta listened as Connie poured out her emotions.

"I thought this would be Tony's reaction. Did you think he would marry you?"

Connie grabbed a tissue and wiped her tears. "Yes, I guess I did." She wondered if his reaction would have been different if Mike O'Day did not want to sign them.

Loretta stayed on the phone with her for a couple of hours. She offered to come over but Connie said no. It was getting late and she needed to get some sleep if she wanted to go to work the next day. Work would help keep her mind on other things. When she awoke, she felt terrible. As she climbed out of bed she felt her stomach turn and she ran to the bathroom and heaved into the toilet. Afterward, she washed her face with cold water. Connie looked at herself in the mirror. She was very pale and decided to call in sick today. Jim was understanding and said he hoped she felt better. It was seldom she took off time from work. Not even for vacation. She probably would need a few days after the abortion. She could not tell Jim the truth. Connie rubbed her belly. The thought of something alive in there sent her running back to the toilet.

Chapter twenty three

The next few days were hard to work but Connie managed. Tony had called to find out if she made an appointment. When she told him no, he became irritated. She told him she would make the appointment soon and they discussed the band and Mike O'Day. Connie felt tired of hearing about the band and being signed. She tried to be interested, but in her heart she knew it meant Tony would be going away. Connie noticed he did not mention the usually weekend plans of getting together. When she brought this up he said he did not know what was happening. Towards the end of the week, Rick called to see how she was and to see if she would have dinner with him one more time before he moved. Connie was hesitant on seeing Rick but did not know if she would ever see him again. She agreed to go out with him Friday night.

When Rick showed up at seven o'clock she did not let him in her house. She had not felt like cleaning and knew the place was a disaster. She knew she looked pale and fragile and tried to wear more make-up, but this only made her look more haunting. On the way to the restaurant Connie was quiet.

"Are you sure everything is okay?" Rick asked during dinner.

She looked into his caring eyes she had fallen in love with that now seemed so long ago. Tears started to stream down her face as she tried to cover them with her hands. "Oh Rick, I'm pregnant."

Connie saw Rick's expression turn to pain and knew by Rick's silence that her words must have hurt as if someone had stabbed him in the heart.

He pushed his plate away. "I always thought when you got pregnant, the child would be mine."

"I'm so sorry Rick; I know how this must hurt you. But I'm going to have an abortion and Tony's going on the road. The band got a recording contract," she said sarcastically, waving her hand through the air. Tears started to well up inside.

"I'm sorry, Connie." Rick took her hand in his. I wish I could make all your problems disappear but I cannot. "Is that what this guy wants, for you to have an abortion?"

Connie looked at Rick's hand that held hers, and nodded. "It's really for the best." She took in a deep breath, "I thought you should know. The night you called, I had just found out. That's why I couldn't see you. I was too much of a wreck."

Rick sat and listened as she told him her fears on getting an abortion. "My biggest fear is something terrible will happen and I will never be able to have children." It was strange she could tell Rick this but she could not tell Tony. "Enough about me and my problems. When do you leave?" Connie took the napkin that Rick handed her and wiped her eyes.

"I'm set to go in three days. They're giving me a week to settle in my new place and then I start work."

"I will miss you," Connie said, wishing things were the way they use to be between them. She knew that was now impossible, too much had happened. Rick drove her home after dinner. She had hoped he would kiss her good-bye but he did not. A lump formed in the back of her throat, "I wish you the best of luck, Rick."

"Thanks, I hope things go well for you, Connie." He watched as she walked into her house and then pulled away.

Once inside, Connie could not hold back her tears any longer. Everything was going wrong in her life. She could not stop it. She went to see if there were any messages on her machine. Just one from Loretta, Tony had not even called. He had been avoiding her for the past week. She had called him twice and left a message. He did not return her calls. She realized what a selfish jerk he was. All he cared about was himself and the band. Even now, when she was carrying his child it did not make a difference. She hated herself for not seeing it before. Looking back when they were together, all he wanted to talk about was himself and the band. Connie went to bed. Her cat Misty, curled up next to her as if sensing something was wrong. "At least I have you," she said as she petted her soft fur.

Chapter twenty four

Weeks had passed and Connie still had not heard from Tony. She called his place but there was no answer. She pressed down the receiver and dialed Ted's.

"Tony's not here. I'll tell him you called." Ted replied.

Connie could hear voices in the background and recognized one of them to be Tony's. Her frustration was mounting. How dare he ignore me like this, she thought. She hung up the phone and decided to drive over there and confront him face to face. She grabbed her keys and headed out the door. Fifteen minutes later she spotted Tony's car in Ted's driveway and parked behind it. She walked in the front door and Ted instantly stood up surprised. "Where is he?" she asked in a tone of voice that was more of a growl.

Ted smirked and sat back down in his chair. "Upstairs. The bedroom on the left."

She quickly turned and headed for the room on the

second floor. She pushed the door open that was slightly ajar and gasped. The shades were open and the sun streamed in, making the room very bright. Connie watched in shock as some girl with huge boobs and short blonde hair laid on top of Tony. Instantly, she felt sick to her stomach and wanted to run, but her legs would not move. He was enjoying himself so much he did not notice she was there. She turned and walked down stairs.

Ted greeted her at the bottom of the stairs and steered her toward the couch and gently set her down next to him. "Look," he said, as he put his arm around her. "I hated to do that to you but at least you know what's going on. Tony's the kind of guy that likes variety as far as chicks go. Now take me for instance," Ted moved his hand to Connie's thigh and began to stroke it. "I could be really happy with some one like you."

Connie stood up immediately. "You stay away from me," she yelled, feeling the anger coming out of her pores as if it were steam. "And tell Tony that goes for him, too." She slammed the door so hard behind her it made the whole house shake. Maybe that got Tony's attention, she thought to herself as she took off down the road.

Chapter twenty five

She still had not called a doctor. She kept putting it off for another day. Although she still looked slim, Connie was having problems fitting into her jeans. She would leave the zipper down and wear long shirts to cover her belly. It was late October and the weather was getting colder. Most of the leaves had turned a beautiful orange and red. The winds that blew in with the season seem to remind Connie that there would be changes in all living things. Connie would wear her long jacket when she went out in public. For the most part, Connie stayed inside. She went to work and to the store to buy food. The rest of the time she spent doing things indoors and watching TV. She was putting a load into the wash when Loretta came over. "So, have you called a Doctor yet?" Loretta said. "And I don't want to hear any of your excuses."

Connie had been trying to avoid one of Loretta's speeches. She shook her head no. Loretta picked up the phone. "I brought the number of a clinic." She handed her the phone and piece of paper with the number. "Call them, now." She insisted.

Connie sat and pushed the buttons on her phone hesitantly. When the receptionist answered, Connie told her she needed to make an appointment. She followed by giving her name, the nature of the visit and her phone number. Connie waited as the receptionist looked at the calendar.

"There was a cancellation for today; can you come in at two?" Her voice asked flatly.

"Today?" Immediately Connie felt Loretta nudging her arm and whispering "Yes, say yes." Connie told the woman that would be fine. When Connie put down the receiver, she realized her hand had been shaking.

"I'm sorry I had to do this." Loretta tried to comfort Connie. "But if you're waiting for that fucking asshole to take you it's not going to happen. I heard the band signed the contract and they are long gone from here. The jerk did not even call before he left, did he? You're better off without him; he's nothing but a fucking coward." Loretta's voice became angry. "No decent guy would have left you like this. "I guess I'll tell you now," Loretta lowered her voice. "Sam and I broke up. We got into this huge argument about how Tony was treating you. And can you believe it," Loretta's voice grew louder, "he sided with Tony." Loretta slapped her hands on her thighs in frustration. She stood up and started to pace back and forth as she continued. "Sam actually thinks you got pregnant on purpose to trap Tony. I refuse to have anything more to do with a man that thinks that way. Men are assholes, all of them." Loretta sat down again next to Connie.

"Loretta, I'm so sorry. I know how much Sam meant to you."

"We had different opinions on a lot of things. It's better I found out now what a jerk he was." Tears started cloud her eyes.

"You were right about everything. Tony is a coward. "How could I have been so wrong about a person? And I was going to buy him a new guitar for Christmas."

"You didn't lend him any money did you?"

"No," Connie felt relieved about that. "Although I probably would have, if he had asked."

A few hours later, Connie and Loretta walked into the Clinic. Connie signed in and was handed forms she had to fill out completely. She sat down next to Loretta and noticed a girl about the age of sixteen with dark shoulder length hair sitting across from her. The girl had tears running down her face and appeared to be alone. She noticed Connie watching her and tried to give her a smile. Connie smiled back and went to the receptionist and asked for a box of tissue. She handed it to the young girl and went back to her seat. There were no words spoken but there was a strange understanding between the two. The girl whispered "Thank you" and wiped her eyes. The nurse appeared and said a   name and the girl quickly stood up and followed the nurse to one of the back rooms. Connie's heart went out to the young girl. Like herself, she probably was pregnant and had no one. Connie felt a deep loneliness inside. A feeling that even Loretta's friendship could not reach. The nurse appeared and called Connie. She followed her to a room and the nurse told her to undress. She was given a paper gown to cover herself. Connie handed her the forms that she filled out and waited for the nurse to leave. She quickly undressed and sat on the table, staring at the stirrups. A few minutes later the doctor entered. He looked at the form and asked when her last period was. He then proceeded to examine her.

Connie discussed her situation and told the doctor she thought an abortion was the best solution. He explained the clinic offered counseling and it is required she talk to the counselor before anything was done.

"We want to make sure the decision you make is the one right for you. And whatever that decision is we will help you with it. Upon the examination and the date of your last period, I say you have less than four weeks if you want the abortion. Inform the receptionist of this time and she will schedule you for counseling and we will be able to do the abortion the same day. Do you have any questions?"

Connie shook her head no and after the doctor left she dressed. She made the necessary arrangements and gave the receptionist her insurance card. She handed it back to her and said most insurance companies did not cover this. She would have to pay for it in full on her next visit. She explained further that they may pay for the examination but not the abortion. Connie understood, and set the date for two weeks. She joined Loretta back in the waiting room. She looked to see if the young girl was around but did not see her. Connie waited until they were in her car before telling her everything. "Can you come with me? They said I'll need someone to drive me home."

"Of course I'll come with you. I think it would be a good idea if I spend the night. Just in case you have complications. Christmas is in two months and this whole thing will be over by then."

Connie knew her friend was only trying to get her mind on something else. The thought of Christmas only darkened her mood. Every year she would spend the holidays with Loretta and her family. Then she would spend the evenings with Rick. She never could tell Loretta. It was something too painful for her to discuss. She hated the holidays. It only reminded her that she did not have a family of her own. It was the loneliest time of the year for her. The season always stirred up memories of her parents and that fateful night. This year would be especially painful without Rick. Connie tried to hold back her tears but could not.

Loretta pulled over and held Connie. "Oh, everything will be fine," she said as Connie sobbed into her coat. "This will all be over real soon." Loretta held her friend for a long time.

Chapter twenty six

Connie sat on her living room floor going through old magazines. She was trying to decide which to keep and which to discard. It was late Saturday afternoon when the doorbell rang. Suddenly, she remembered it was Halloween and she did not have any candy for the kids. Maybe they will go away if I do not answer it. The doorbell rang again. "Oh, I'm coming, I'm coming." She quickly went to the door and opened it.

"Trick or treat."

Connie looked down and saw the most adorable little girl with dark hair and twinkling eyes, dressed in a princess costume. She was holding out a bag that was as big as she was. "And what are you?" Connie asked.

"Go on Trisha, tell her." The Mother coaxed. The little girl turned to her Mother and giggled. She turned back to Connie.

"Princess," she giggled again.

"Well you're a very pretty princess." Connie looked up at the mother whose face was beaming with love for the child. "Wait right here," Connie hurried to grab her purse and went back to the door and slipped a dollar into the little girl's bag.

The Mother laughed, "I suggest you go to the store and buy candy or you will be broke before the night ends."

Connie smiled. "Yes, I think I will," The little girl said thank-you, and Connie closed the door. Connie grabbed her purse and her jacket and drove to the nearest store. The little girl's face stayed on her mind. She wondered if the child she was carrying was a girl or a boy. A tingling feeling came over her. I could have a little girl like her. "No, Connie, you have to be out of your mind," she said loudly. She thought of raising a child herself. She tried to envision herself as a mother. She pulled into the shopping center and ran inside. She grabbed three bags of assorted candies and found herself watching every mother and child in the store. She paid for the candy and drove back home and poured the candy into a bowl. Every time the doorbell rang, she looked forward to answering the door. She had never paid much attention to children before. Suddenly, a whole new world was opening up to he, and Connie pondered the possibilities. I could afford to raise a child alone. Having a child would hinder my freedom somewhat. At times I would need a sitter. This house is big enough; I could take my parents room and turn my room into a nursery. The black cloud that hovered over Connie for so long seemed to lighten. She envisioned a little one running around. A child she could take care of. Someone to buy toys for, and most of all, someone to share her life with. Someone to love.

Chapter twenty seven

"Are you crazy?" Loretta screamed, as she jumped up and started to pace back and forth. She had hurried over when Connie called and asked if they could talk about something right away. Connie would not give her any hints but said it was very important and would only discuss it in person. "I can't believe what I'm hearing. Did you fall down and hit your head, or what? You don't know one thing about babies." Loretta's voice grew louder. "Do you know what everyone in town will be saying? Mrs. Evans will have a field day with this. I can hear her now, telling everyone that comes in to buy their morning donuts. Did you hear about poor Connie Wade? She got herself pregnant and her boyfriend took a hike. She will probably tell the town it's Rick's. Loretta sat back on Connie's couch and took a deep breath. "I don't think you have thought about this all the way through. Are you doing this hoping it will bring Tony back?"

Connie felt her anger rise and now she stood up to pace the room. "This has nothing to do with Tony," she yelled as she waved her hand through the air. "This has to do with me. I don't care what the people of Greenville say. I want this baby more than I ever wanted anything else. This is a decision I have to make, not you. This will affect my life, not yours. People have always taken care of me and made decisions for me ever since my parents died. My lawyer, your parents, you, Rick. Do not think I'm not grateful," she quickly added. "I love your parents," her voice softened. "If it weren't for them I probably would have ended up in some orphanage. I need to start making my own decisions. Can you understand that? You have always influenced my decisions but I'm not going to let you do it this time." Tears came to Connie's pleading eyes. "You have a family to love, I do not. I need someone to love." Connie looked at her friend, begging her to understand.

"But my family is your family. You're like a sister. Mom and dad love you like a daughter."

Connie sat down next to Loretta and looked into her friends frowning face. "I know that, and I love you and your family too, but I guess I just can't explain it. All I know is this baby is part of me and I want it very, very much.

"I don't think you've ever stood up to me like this before." Loretta sat quietly for some time staring at the wall. "To raise a child with two parents is difficult enough, but to raise one alone?" She ran her hands through her red hair before facing Connie. "Can I be the God Mother?"

Tears came to Connie's eyes. "Of course, who else

would I choose." Connie hugged Loretta and felt relieved. "I thought my decision might have cost me our friendship."

"Are you kidding, you're going to need me more than ever. This child is going to be so spoiled," Loretta wiped the tears from her eyes.

"Come on, I want to show you what I have in mind for the nursery."

Chapter twenty eight

"Debbie, I have left the number of the ranch next to the phone," Connie said as she pulled her long black hair back into a ponytail.

"Don't worry about a thing. Trisha's going to watch this movie with me, aren't you?" Debbie tickled the little girl sitting next to her on the couch.

Connie smiled as she heard her two year old daughter squeal with laughter. She was an exceptionally beautiful child. Trisha had inherited Connie's dark hair and Tony's blue eyes. She will definitely turn heads when she grows up, Connie thought proudly. She had not seen or heard from Tony since that one day she found him at Ted's with that girl. The band was releasing their second album, and Connie would sometimes read about them in those trashy newspapers at the checkout stands. One time it showed Tony's picture with a beautiful girl on his arm. The article said she was a model from France. It did not hurt her to see

Tony with other women. What hurt was the fact he did not care about Trisha. She knew someday her little girl would ask questions about her father. What could she say? I am sorry darling; your father was a totally selfish man and a jerk. The only thing he ever cared about was becoming a rock star. By the time I figured it out, I was pregnant with you. Would she go on to tell her Tony wanted her to have an abortion? She was so glad she did not. It would have been the biggest mistake of her life. The love she felt for her daughter was the most powerful feeling she ever experienced.

"Mommy," Trisha ran to her side. "I want to go horsy ride too."

Connie reached down and picked up her daughter. "You can go when you're a big girl. Connie watched as her daughter's face began to frown. "Oh no, you're not getting your way this time." She set her down on the floor. "You be a good girl." Trisha walked over to her toys on the floor and began to play. A few minutes later she seemed so engrossed in them she did not hear her mother walk out the door.

After Connie had Trisha she started going up to the ranch again to ride. She found it helped take the pressure off her of being a single mom. It was soothing to ride through the woods and hear nothing but the sound of the horse's hooves. On this day she rode over to the clearing by the creek. This was her favorite spot. She dismounted and tied the reins to a nearby branch. As she sat, she took off her boots and socks and dipped her feet into the cold water.

She looked over at her horse and watched as he would eat a few strands of grass and then drink from the creek. Suddenly his ears went back as he turned his head in the direction of the path leading to the area. A second later Connie heard the hooves of another horse approaching. She had never seen anyone else come here and it startled her. She watched as a tall figure of a man riding came through the woods approached. The rider stopped at the end of the trail when he saw her. "Rick," Connie's eyes widened from the shock. She saw his warm smile greet her as he dismounted and tied his horse up next to hers. "I cannot believe it's you," she said as he came nearer. "How did you know I was here?" He looked good, she thought. His face, darkened by the sun, enhanced his beautiful dark eyelashes. His black hair was cut short with a few strands out of place from the ride. He still wore his shirts tucked in tight with the first three buttons undone revealing his hairy chest. His blue jeans always looked as if they were tailor made for him. His black riding boots were spotless, as he always had kept them clean. Rick sat next to her.

"It wasn't hard, Trisha's sitter said you went riding and I remembered this was your favorite place." Rick looked into her eyes. "You are still as beautiful as ever."

"It's good to see you Rick. I can't tell you how many times I wanted to pick up the phone and call you."

"What stopped you?"

Connie shrugged her shoulders. "The thought you might be involved with someone. I thought you might hang up on me."

"I would never hang up on you.   And as for being involved," Rick hesitated. "I was engaged until she decided to break up with me two months ago."

"I'm sorry, Rick. That must have been very painful for you. And after what I did to you."

"That's why she wouldn't marry me."

"I don't understand. Rick. Why would I have anything to do with her decision to break up with you?"

"I was honest with her. I told her I was still very much in love with you and would always wonder if things could have worked out if I had stayed." He grabbed a few stones and threw them into the creek, apprehensive of Connie's reaction.

Tears welled up inside Connie as she looked into Rick's sweet brown eyes that always seem to sparkle. "How could I have hurt you the way that I did? Things got so out of hand and by the time I realized it, I was pregnant and you were gone." Connie wiped the tears from her eyes. "How could I have come to you and say I'm sorry. It was too late."

"It's never too late," Rick said tenderly, looking at her. "Not if two people still love each other." Rick hesitated. "Do you, Connie? Do you still love me?" His eyes searched hers for the answer to the question he needed to know.

"I've never stopped loving you, Rick." Connie put her hand over his.

Rick smiled. "Then marry me," he said softly. "I know in my heart you're the only one that can make me happy. And there will never be anyone I love as deeply as I do you."

Connie smiled. "You know this is a package deal here. And I have to warn you, Trisha can be very demanding at times."

"I realize I'll have to share you, but it's better than not having you at all. It will work out; I know it will," Rick pleaded. "I'll be a good father to Trisha."

Connie held her hand up to his face. "Then I will." She knew in her heart it was the right thing to do. We were meant to be together. She wanted to spend the rest of her life making him happy.

Rick pulled her closer whispering into her ear. "I have missed you so," he said as he kissed her neck.

Connie closed her eyes and moaned. She felt Rick's lips meet hers as he gently laid her down in the grass. She quickly unbuttoned his shirt so she could caress his bare back. The familiar softness of his skin felt good to her touch. His hands reached for her breasts as he gently took off her clothes. She trembled with excitement as she felt his hardness against her. Connie watched his hand between her legs massaging her to near climax. She felt his lips licking her nipples to ecstasy. "Take me now," she whispered. Rick spread her legs and gently entered her. Connie felt a searing pain as if she were losing her virginity all over again. She had not made love to a man in years. The pain soon turned into mounting pleasure. She felt her body respond very quickly. She held Rick closer and arched her back as he penetrated her even deeper. His thrusts grew faster, bringing them both to a tense climax.

They held each other until dusk and then rode back to the ranch.

Chapter twenty nine

Connie looked at her image in the mirror. Her wedding gown was the most beautiful gown she had ever seen. The white satin dress had laced mixed with sequins and the low cut front revealing just enough cleavage. She decided not to curl her long dark hair and let it hang. "I'm so glad I went with this dress."

"I told you so." Loretta said with a smile. "Now where is the veil? It's almost time." Loretta looked around the room and spotted it near the box of shoes. She quickly walked over and grabbed the veil. Her long green chiffon dress made a swishing sound as she walked. She helped Connie adjust it on her head. "There." She stood back and admired her friend. "You look beautiful." Tears started to come to Loretta's eyes.

"Connie saw her friend's reflection in the mirror. "Don't get me started," she warned. "We've worked too hard on our make-up to have it ruined by tears."

The pastor's wife, Betty, knocked gently on the door. "Are you ready my dear," she asked. "It's almost one." Betty, now in her sixties, knew Connie since she was born. She and her husband had christened Connie when she was a baby. They had her parent's funeral service in their church. She had watched Connie grow into a beautiful young lady.

Connie let out a sigh. "We're ready." She turned and picked up her flowers and followed Betty and Loretta out into the hall. She waited for Betty to take her place at the organ. Betty then proceeded to play the wedding march. Loretta turned to her and gave her a quick hug before she started her walk down the isle. She waited until Loretta was at a certain pew before following. The church was half filled with people she and Rick had known their whole lives. Many of them were town folks. Even Mrs. Evans from the bakery had come. When Connie had invited her all she could say was "It's about time that man does the right thing by you." She chose to believe Trisha was Rick's. She saw Trisha smiling as she sat in between Loretta's parents, Mary and Dave. In the year that Rick had come back into her life Trisha had grown to love him. He would often tickle her and she would squeal with delight. She had reached the altar now and turned to look at Rick. He was so handsome in his black tuxedo. He smiled as he took her hand in his and repeated his wedding vows to her.

"I promise to love, honor, and cherish you, till death do us part." Rick said.

Connie could not contain her tears of joy as she said her vows. The love in her heart for the man she thought she had lost forever would now be her husband. She wanted to spend the rest of her life making him happy.

"I pronounce you man and wife." The pastor closed his book and smiled at Rick and Connie.

Rick gently lifted her veil and kissed her. The room filled with noise as they all proceeded out of the church to wait for the newly wed couple.

Once outside, handfuls of birdseed were thrown at them. The pastor said he preferred that to rice. The rice could choke the birds that would always flock down and eat after the services.

"Mommy," Trisha ran into Connie's arms. "I was a good girl. I didn't cry."

"Yes, you were," Connie said as she picked up her daughter. "I'm so proud of you." Connie kissed her little girl on the cheek.

"Grandma cried. I saw her. Can we have some cake now?"

Connie laughed as she ran her fingers through her daughter's dark curls.

"Soon," Rick smiled as he gently pinched her cheek. "Don't you want to go for a ride around town and honk at everyone we see?"

"Yeah!" Trisha's eyes grew wide with excitement.

"It sure turned out to be a beautiful day for your wedding," Mary said.

Connie looked at the blue skies and agreed. "It rained all

day yesterday; I wasn't sure how it was going to be." A few more people surrounded them offering their congratulations. Rick's parents came up and kissed Connie on the cheek, along with his brother Ron. He was a few years younger than Rick but looked just like him.

"Let's go, Mommy," Trisha wined. "I want to honk at everyone."

"Okay. Okay." Connie looked at Rick and smiled. "This was your idea, not mine." She turned back to Mary and Dave. "We will see you at the hall." She put Trisha down and led the way towards the car that was especially decorated for them. Ron got behind the wheel and Trisha sat next to him. Loretta sat up front. Rick and Connie sat close to each other in the back seat. There was a huge sign tied on the trunk saying "Just Married." Streamers were taped to all sides of the car. Trisha reached over and started honking the horn.

"Loretta laughed as she turned to Rick and Connie in the back seat. "She knows her part well."

They drove around town as people they knew on the streets smiled and waved. Rick took Connie's hand in his as he leaned over to kiss her. Soon they changed direction and headed for the hall where the reception was being held. The large room seemed filled with square tables that were decorated with white tablecloths, and each had a candle in the middle. At the end of the room several tables were put together and decorated especially for the bride and groom and their party. Off to the side was the three-tiered wedding cake Mrs. Evans baked for Connie. It was her gift to them. On the other side of the room was the band. They were still setting up when the guests started to arrive. Connie and Rick took their seats. Trisha sat between Connie and Loretta.

Soon the evening was in full swing. After dinner was served the girl that was one of the singers in the band went up to the mike.

"May I have you're attention, please." The room became quiet as all eyes turned to the beautiful blonde with the sweet voice. "We would like to play this first song from Rick to Connie. Please come up here." She watched as Rick and Connie walked to the dance floor. The singer spoke into the mike as she looked at Connie. "I don't think he will mind if I tell you what he told me. He said every time he heard this song he thought of you, Connie." The band started the introduction to their song. Rick took Connie into his arms and smiled as they began to dance.

"I'm so happy you came back to me Rick," Connie whispered into his ear. "I thought I lost you forever." The song ended and Rick kissed her gently on the lips. The band broke into another song and more couples joined them on the dance floor. Afterwards, the photographer took their picture cutting the cake. Then Ron went over to the mike and asked for everyone's attention.

"I just want to say I think the two of you have a love that is special. And I wish you both the very best." He lifted his glass to Connie and Rick. Everyone in the room raised their glasses for the toast and returned to their conversations.

"I wished your parents could have been here to see your wedding." Mary said to Connie as she held Trisha's hand. "They would have been so proud of you, my dear. Just as proud as I am."

Connie gave her a hug. "I'm sure they were here in spirit.

Mary looked down to see Trisha yawn. "I think we'll be leaving soon. She's getting tired."

"Why can't I go with you and Rick?" Trisha wined as she rubbed her eyes.

Connie recognized her daughter's pouting face and reached down to pick up Trisha. "Don't you want to go with grandma and grandpa? You will have so much fun this week. Their going to take you to the zoo and to the beach, all sorts of fun things. I bet you won't even miss me."

"Yes I will," she retorted stubbornly.

Connie's heart ached as she kissed her daughter's cheek. She had never been apart from Trisha more than a few hours a day while she worked, including the times she and Rick went out riding or to dinner.

Connie swallowed the lump that began to form in her throat. "I want you to be a good girl for Mommy, okay?" Trisha nodded as Connie gave her to Mary.

"It looks like someone's tired." Rick teased as he walked up to Connie.

"She's not the only one," Dave slurred. "It was a beautiful wedding my dear. Mom, you better drive us home," he said as he handed his wife the car keys.

"No problem," she replied as she took the keys from her husband. "We better tell Loretta we're going. Call us when you get to the resort."

"I will," Connie kissed Trisha one more time before they left to talk to Loretta.

"She'll be fine." Rick said as he put his arm around Connie. "They'll take good care of her."

"I know," Connie said. "We should be leaving soon, too. We have an early flight tomorrow."

"Yes, I cannot wait," he grinned. "I've always wanted to take you to Hawaii. The island is a spectacular sight."

Chapter thirty

The weather was very hot as they got off the plane at Honolulu International Airport. Rick and Connie collected their luggage and hailed a cab to take them to the resort where they would be spending the week.

"Aloha. Is this the first time to the Islands?" the driver asked as he pulled out into traffic.

"Yes," Rick replied. "We're on our honeymoon."

"Ah, then you must go to the north shore beaches. They are remote and romantic. Tomorrow morning they have tours that go up to Diamond Head." The driver pointed toward the mountain. There are lots of things to do, you won't be bored." The cab driver grinned as his eyes looked in the rearview mirror.

"It's beautiful here." Connie said looking toward Mamala Bay and seeing the clear blue water with its white caps rushing to the shore. She smelled the fresh ocean waters and watched the palm trees sway in the wind along the beaches. The mountain sights were spectacular.

"Were you born here?" Rick asked the driver.

"Yes, my family has been here for three generations. I wouldn't be happy anywhere else." He pulled into the parking lot of the resort that faced Waikiki Beach. He retrieved their luggage from the trunk.

Rick handed him some bills.

"Mahalo, and hauoli maoli oe." The cab driver smiled. It means thank you, and here's to your happiness.

"Thank you," he said before following Connie inside. The cool air conditioning was a relief from the heat outside. Rick and Connie walked up to the counter and set the luggage on the floor. "We have reservations."

The man who also looked like a local smiled. "Aloha," he said and gave Rick a key. "I hope your stay is a pleasurable one. If you need anything, let us know."

"Can you tell me where the car rental place is?" Rick asked.

The desk clerk pointed across the street. "I hope you made reservations."

Rick smiled. "We did." He turned and picked up the luggage and walked off to find their room. "Here we are." Rick set the luggage down and used the key to open the door. He then turned to Connie and kissed her lightly on the lips before picking her up and carrying her into the room. He gently laid her on the bed and kissed her again.

Connie giggled. "Are you planning to make love to me now with the door wide open and our luggage in the hall?" she teased.

Rick smiled, "I suppose that would get us kicked out of here, wouldn't it?" He walked over to the door and retrieved the luggage and closed the door behind him.

Connie was standing at the window watching the view. Her long dark hair pulled back in a ponytail. "It's beautiful here, isn't it? It's as if there is no end to the ocean. It seems to go on forever and ever." Far off in the distance she could see people riding out the waves on surfboards. Even further out were sailing boats.

Rick walked up behind her and put his arms around her waist. "You are beautiful," he said as he kissed her neck. His hands reached up to her breasts as he caressed them gently.

Connie moaned softly as she turned to face him, her lips meeting his. Her body fert his warmth, his hardness. Her body responded to his as he slipped his fingers down her shorts between her legs. Her hands felt his soft skin under his shirt. They quickly undressed and fell on top of the bed in their urgency to be as one. Connie's body trembled with excitement as Rick's tongue trailed down between her legs. He then entered her, and with each thrust her moans grew louder, bringing her nearer to climax until the electrical moment exploded inside her. "Oh, Rick," she said lying in his arms. "That was wonderful." She could not tell him that was her first orgasm she had with him. He kissed her and held her in his arms as they both fell asleep.

Chapter thirty one

Rick and Connie picked up the car rental and started the drive up to Nuuannu Pali Lookout. Rick parked and locked the car. There were signs posted warning people not to leave car doors open. They followed the trail leading to the most spectacular sights Connie had ever seen. From the jagged cliffs you could see the clouds hover over the valley meeting the blue skies of the horizon. Connie could feel the strong winds chill her to the bone. She wrapped her arms around her waist to keep warm.

"Do you want to go back to the car?" Rick asked.

"No." She smiled at him and returned to the view. "I'm fine. The view is worth the cold; we might never get the chance to see anything this beautiful again."

Rick took the camera he brought with him and snapped a picture of Connie looking over the horizon. Her long black hair was thrown in every direction from the wind. Her cheeks were red from the cold. They stood there for a while watching the clouds move in from the ocean. A young beautiful woman who looked to be in her twenties joined them to watch the view. She looked like a local and turned to Connie and smiled.

"Lani," she said, returning her gaze to the sky.

"I'm sorry. What did you say?" Connie asked.

"Lani." The woman's voice was soft. "It means heaven." Connie smiled at the woman, "Lani," she said. The woman stayed a few minutes more and headed down towards the path. Soon Rick and Connie left. "That's strange," Connie noticed when they were almost to the car. "She's gone. She couldn't have been more than a half a minute ahead of us."

"Maybe she took another path." Rick said.

"I didn't see another path, did you?"

Rick shrugged. "Do you want to look for her?"

"No, I just thought it was strange. "Let's go get something to eat. All this fresh air has made me hungry." The next day they hiked three miles to the summit of Diamond Head, exploring the dark underground passages near the peak. Afterward, they went swimming and stayed on the beach to watch the amber colors reflect off the waters as the sun set.

"Look how dark you've gotten," Connie said, watching Rick undress from his suit. "You're beginning to look like a local. I'm going to call Trisha before she goes to bed." Connie sat on the side of the bed and dialed the familiar number. "It's beautiful here, Mary. You and Dave should come here sometime." Connie filled her in on all the exciting things she had seen and how friendly people seemed to be. "Can I talk to Trisha?" She waited on the line until she heard her daughter's voice say, "Hello?" "Hi, honey. Mommy's coming home in two days. I miss you. Hugs and kisses, Trisha. Put Grandma back on. I'll see you soon. Mary, we should be in at 2 p.m. at O'Hare airport. We'll see you then." Connie hung up the phone and felt depressed. Hearing her daughter's voice made her miss her even more.

Rick sat down next to Connie. "You miss her, don't you? We'll be home soon. I can't wait to see her face when she sees all the toys you bought her. Do you think they'll let us on the plane with all this stuff?" Rick teased.

Connie looked at all the bags stacked in the corner and smiled. "I guess I did go a little overboard." Every time they had passed a souvenir shop Connie would run in to look for something for Trisha.

Rick watched the far away look come into Connie's eyes. "Come on," he said to get her attention. "Let's go eat."

Connie had a taste for steak, so they dinned at a restaurant that served American and Pacific cuisine. Afterward, they went to see a traditional luau. The huge stage was outdoors. Behind it, a fountain of water rose from the ground that with lighting, creating an orange glow on the dancers. The audience could feel the cool breezes from the ocean as they watched and listened to the one hundred performers tell the history of the islands. When the show ended, Connie and Rick went back to their room and made love. Again, Connie felt herself tremble with excitement as she reached heights of pleasure she never thought she would reach.

Rick held her in his arms. "We only have one more day here."

"I know," she said, her voice sounding sad. "This whole week seems like a beautiful dream."

"What should we do on our last day?" Rick asked as he squeezed her gently.

"We haven't gone horse back riding yet."

"Then that's what we will do." Rick held Connie in his arms until they fell asleep.

Chapter thirty-two

Connie rushed through the store after finding Trisha's last Christmas present. Connie had seen the advertisement in the paper and knew her little girl would love it. It was an adorable cuddly stuffed teddy bear with long eyelashes. It wore a pink and white-stripped dress and had a matching umbrella. She told Rick she would be home by eight and it was nearly that now. She had not expected the stores to be crowded so soon, Christmas was still four weeks away. Connie looked for the shortest line and darted towards it. Five people remained in front of her. I will never get out of here, she thought. She looked in her cart at the teddy bear and knew in her heart it would be worth the wait when Trisha opened it on Christmas morning. Her little girl was now seven years old. The image of her face popped into Connie's mind. Trisha made her life meaningful and gave her happiness that she never thought existed. Anticipating Trisha's excitement over Christmas gave Connie so much to look forward to. For years following her parent's death she would dread the holidays. Now she could not wait for them. Rick had made her life complete. They had celebrated their third anniversary last summer. Even though Rick adored Trisha, Connie was eager to carry Rick's baby. Each month they hoped and each month there would be disappointment. Rick started to wear loose fitting underwear and jeans. Loretta had read an article somewhere stating this might help the male produce more sperm. So far it did not work. Connie's eyes fell on the box of Christmas cards she was purchasing. She would buy a special one for Rick. She always did.

It was finally Connie's turn at the check out counter. She took the items out of the cart and placed them on the conveyer to be scanned. She wrote out a check for the amount and grabbed the bags and headed out to her car. Once outside she noticed the whether had changed. The snow that had been coming down lightly a while ago was now heavier. The wind gusts were stronger, making visibility difficult. Connie threw the bag into the back seat and grabbed a brush to clear her windows. By the time she cleared off the front she had to redo the back again before pulling out of the parking lot. She fastened her seat belt and turned the defroster on high, hoping this would help her to see. Under her feet was a puddle of wet snow from her boots. Her gloves were soaked to the skin, leaving her hands cold and wet. She waited until the car became warmer before taking them off. Connie could feel and hear the strength of the wind as she pulled out of the parking lot.

This is a storm, she thought to herself. I do not recall the weatherman saying anything about this. She reached for the radio and listened to the local station.

"There are storm warnings in effect," the announcer said. "Fifty mile per hour winds are being reported in McHenry county. The National Weather Service is advising people to stay inside. Some roads have been closed." There was a shuffle of papers being heard before the announcer continued. "Randall, Route 47, Route14....

"Route 14," Connie's heart began to pound. That's the road I am on now, she thought. The snow was so heavy; Connie could not tell where the road was anymore. Everything was white. Miles of open farmland on both sides of the road made the blowing snow worse. Connie was frightened. She had not seen a car in either direction for some time. Years ago, Rick tried to persuade her to buy a cellular phone. He seemed worried she might become stranded out here in the boonies. At the time, she ignored him. Now she wished she had one. She looked down at her speedometer. She was doing thirty in a fifty-five. She spotted headlights in her rearview mirror and felt a little better. At least if this road was closed she would not be alone. She wondered if she should turn around and take an alternate road, but that would take her twenty minutes out of her way. Connie looked in her rearview mirror and noticed the car behind her was approaching her very quickly. In a few minutes she realized the vehicle was a truck and not a car. The driver began to honk and Connie could hear yelling as they pulled up beside her. She unrolled her window and saw they were two teenage boys.

"Hey baby," a boy with sandy brown hair yelled. He took a sip from a beer bottle. "What are you doing out here? Are you lost?"

The driver howled, "You want a beer?" He reached for a bottle and handed it to his friend. "Throw it to her, man," he slurred.

Connie quickly rolled up her window just as he tossed the bottle. She heard the glass break and leaned to the right as to avoid the shattering glass. Her left hand that held the steering wheel felt a stabbing pain. Connie looked down for an instant and saw a piece of glass sticking out of her hand. She let out a gasp. Blood was oozing from the wound. She felt frightened now and her heart began to pound. She pushed her foot down on the accelerator and her car sped ahead of the two boys in the truck. They had better traction and sped up right behind her honking again and flashing the bright lights on her. Connie could see the boy that threw the bottle waving another one in the air as the driver continued to howl. Connie gripped the steering wheel tightly as her hands began to shake. Only if someone else would be on this road I might have a chance, she thought. She searched for on coming cars but there were none. Connie felt the truck bump her from behind. She put her foot down on the accelerator causing her to lose control. She sharply turned the steering wheel in the direction of the spin, causing the car to go sideways. Her screams filled the silence of the night as she watched in horror as the truck's headlights slammed into the driver's side.

Chapter thirty three

"Oh Mom," Loretta ran into her arms as she saw her parents step out of the elevator. "They are not sure if Connie's going to make it," Loretta sobbed. "Her heart stopped once and the doctor said she has a lot of internal injuries. They have her in surgery now."

"Is Rick here?" Mary asked, guiding her daughter to a nearby seat.

"Yes, he's down the hall with Trisha. He is a wreck. "I can't believe this is happening again." Loretta's mother stared at the familiar white walls of the emergency room. She turned her gaze toward her husband, Dave. "Can you...?"

"No, I can't," his voice becoming angry as he clenched his fists. "I'd like to know where those two idiots are that caused this."

Loretta could see the hatred in her father's green eyes as he looked to her for an answer. She was proud of the fact that her mother and father had accepted Connie as their own on that fatal night she had lost her parents. There was never a question of who was to raise Connie. If anyone else would have tried, her parents would have fought them for that right. After all, Bill and Catherine had chosen them to be Connie's godparents. They were Trisha's grandparents. Loretta noticed he was still wearing his white shirt and striped tie from work. He had just gotten home when she called from the hospital to tell them what happened. "Those idiots were treated and released into police custody. Everyone here could tell they were drunk. I heard the officer telling another officer it's probably what saved them from being injured, plus the fact they were in a truck." Loretta wiped her nose with a tissue.

"Pull yourself together," Mary said to her daughter. "You can't let Trisha see you like this. Maybe we should take her home with us for now. Take us to Rick and see what he says." They followed Loretta around the corner to the waiting area.

Rick had his head in his hands and was sobbing. Trisha stood next to him, looking confused.

"Rick," Dave said as he put his hand on his shoulder. "Mary thinks we should take Trisha home with us. What do you think?"

"No," Trisha protested inching closer to Rick. "I want to stay here."

Rick looked up to see the doctor coming toward him. He instantly stood up to greet him.

"Rick," the doctor's face beaded with perspiration.

"Connie's in the recovery room. We have done everything we could. The next twenty-four hours are critical."

The doctor went on to explain about her internal injuries but Rick went numb. He heard Loretta sob and saw Mary go to her daughter's side. "I must see her." He followed the doctor to the room and watched as a machine breathed life into Connie's lungs. Another machine monitored her heartbeat. Her head was bandaged and her right eye looked black and blue. A tube ran from her arm as she lay unconscious.

Rick gently sat next to her and held her hand. "Tears flowed from his eyes. "Oh, Connie," he wept. "Please don't leave me. I can't live without you."

"She's going to make it, Rick." Mary stood beside him and watched as Connie lay there. "Trisha's in the waiting room. I am taking her home with us. Call us if there is the slightest change."

Rick nodded. "I will Mary."

"Are you staying?" Mary turned to Loretta.

Loretta dabbed at her eyes with a tissue and nodded. Her Mother was always a strong person when it came to emergencies. Loretta wished she had her strength right now. She watched as her mother met her father and Trisha outside the room. Like Rick, she thought it best not to let Trisha see how worried they were. She was only seven. Loretta waited until they left and approached the nurse at the desk. "Excuse me; is there a chapel in the hospital?"

The young nurse smiled. "Yes, it's on the first floor. You'll see the sign as soon as you get off the elevator."

"Thank you," Loretta said. She followed the signs and entered the small chapel. Loretta felt relieved to find no one else there. She made the cross gesture with her hand before kneeling. Tears came to her eyes as she whispered. "Please, God, don't let Connie die. Her family needs her. I need her."

Chapter thirty four

Rick suddenly awoke when he felt Connie's hand stir in his. He had fallen asleep in a chair next to the bed. "Connie, I'm here." He squeezed her hand gently. Her one eye that was not black and blue opened slightly.

"Rick," she mumbled as she tried to focus. Her whole body hurt, especially her head.

"Don't talk; you're going to be okay."

"Rick." The pain was so immense. "Promise me," she whispered, "promise me you will take care of Trisha."

"Do not say that," Rick pleaded. "You're going to be fine. You'll probably be home in a---

"Promise me." Connie's hand went limp in Rick's. The heart monitor gave off a steady beep.

Rick instantly stood over her, tears streaming down his face. "Connie," he yelled. "Please don't leave me, please. I love you."

A nurse followed by a doctor rushed into the room. "Sir,

please wait out side." The nurse moved a serving table out of the way and the doctor bent over Connie to examine her. Two more people entered the door and rushed to Connie's side.

"Do not let her die," Rick begged the nurse as he left the room. He watched in terror as the doctor and nurses worked on Connie. One nurse closed the door behind him and he no longer could see what they were doing. He stood there, feeling numb. Part of him believing none of this was real. This is not happening, he thought. Another nurse came up to Rick.

"Please sir, go to the waiting room. We'll be with you as soon as we can."

Rick slowly walked to the area and saw Loretta asleep on the couch. He sat down next to her, unsure if he should wake her or not. Maybe he thought if she wakes up he'll find out this is not happening. His thoughts went back to seeing Connie lying in bed with all those tubes hooked up to her. His mind raced back to the previous day. They woke up and he made love to her, hoping this time they would conceive. Later that day he walked into the kitchen and she was standing by the sink doing dishes. He came up to her putting his arms around her. She smiled, kissing him lightly on the lips. The twinkle in her eyes as she whispered to him of her plans to go Christmas shopping. He remembered thinking how beautiful she looked. Why didn't he tell her that? When the last time he told her how much he loved her? How could he go on without her? Then came the memory of the police coming to the door and telling him that Connie was in an accident flooded in.

"Rick," the doctor said as he stood next to him.

Rick's mind flew back to the present as he heard the doctor's voice.

"I'm sorry, we did our best but the internal damage was too severe."

"Please, God. Don't let this be true." Rick sobbed not wanting to accept this. He could hear Loretta crying beside him. "How do I tell Trisha her mommy's gone and she is not coming back?" Rick remembered Connie's last wish.

Chapter thirty five

Rick barely heard the reverend say his final words at the funeral home. He stared at the mauve coffin with gold handles, red and white roses surrounded Connie. Even though they never discussed it, Rick thought it best to have Connie buried next to her parents. He stood holding Trisha's hand and listened as she gently cried over the loss of her mother. She had come to him this morning with her hairbrush asking him to fix her hair. Connie had always pinned it back with a pink barrette. He had tried his best but it looked in disarray. Trisha seemed to sense his thoughts.

She turned to him and said. Don't worry. You'll get the hang of it."

His heart went out to the little girl he would now be raising on his own. Although he had a hard time expressing it, he loved Trisha very much. He took her into his arms and hugged her, fighting his pain deep inside.

It seemed as if the whole town showed up, people Connie had known her whole life. The reverend that baptized her and married her and Rick handled the service. Each time someone came up and offered their condolences, Rick would feel his throat tighten. He could only whisper his thanks.

Because of the extent of her head injuries, the coroner thought it would be best to have a closed casket. On a table nearby was a picture of Connie Rick had given to the coroner to be displayed. It was a picture that Rick took when they were in Hawaii on top of Nuuannu Pali Lookout. He remembered thinking he had never seen her look more beautiful, the wind blowing her hair back and her sweet smile as she gazed at him. His heart ached at the thought of living his life without her. All he ever wanted was for them to be together, to raise Trisha and to have a child of their own someday. Now that dream was gone forever. Thanks to those punk kids, he thought. They are in jail for now until the bonds set. Anger built up inside him every time someone would mention the two boys that were responsible for taking Connie's life. Steve Carson, the police officer that was handling the case, grew up with him. He had confided in Rick the day before and said the passenger of the other car said they were just out having fun. That infuriated Rick more. "I want them to pay for this," he yelled to Steve.

"Are you coming with us, Rick?" Mary said, walking up to Rick. "Most of the people are coming by our house."

"No, Mary," Rick realized the service was over and he

had been staring at the coffin. "I think I'll go home and try to sleep. Can you take Trisha?"

"I want to go with you, Rick," Trisha said, not letting go of Rick's hand. "Mommy said I'm to stay with you."

Rick looked down at Trisha's defiant face. He could see the confused look on Mary's face. He shrugged his shoulders, taking it as something Connie had once said to her. "I guess I'll take her with me." Before leaving, more people came up to him giving their condolences and asking if they can be of any help to call. Loretta kissed Rick on the cheek and said she would be in touch. Rick took a final look at the coffin and felt awful leaving Connie there. For years she had been at his side. He took Trisha's hand and they headed for home. He fixed a sandwich for Trisha and himself, and then went to lie down in the bedroom. He turned to face the side of the bed Connie slept in, remembering the times they would make love. He quickly got out of bed and went down to the kitchen and grabbed the bottle of vodka from the cabinet. He poured himself a drink and sat at the table. Hours passed as one drink turned into half a bottle. He barely noticed when Trisha came in and said goodnight. He soon realized he was dozing off and staggered to the couch where he finally was able to sleep.

Chapter Thirty six

"Hi. We're not able to come to the phone right now, but if you leave your name…" "Connie," Rick called, sitting up straight, his head suddenly throbbing. He then realized it was Connie's voice on the answering machine. Someone had called and hung up on him. Rick went over to the machine and disconnected it. He then went into the kitchen and grabbed a couple of aspirins and swallowed them with a glass of water. He looked at the sink of dirty dishes and walked back into the living room where he sat and stared at the TV that was not on. It was about ten in the morning when Trisha came downstairs.

"Rick," she said, tugging at his sleeve. "I'm hungry."

"Well go fix yourself something to eat," he snapped.

"But Mommy always fixed me breakfast and she said now you have to."

"Quit playing these games Trisha." Rick said sternly. "Mommy is not here, and it's about time you start doing things on your own. You're perfectly capable of fixing yourself a bowl of cereal.

Tears started down Trisha's face as she walked away from Rick. She went into the kitchen and moved one of the chairs over to the cabinet. She stood on a chair and retrieved the box of cereal and then moved the chair to another cabinet for one of the remaining clean bowls. She took the milk from the refrigerator and poured it, spilling some on the table. She then added the cereal also spilling it. After getting a spoon, she sat down to eat. When she finished, she put her dirty dish in the sink and went in the living room and turned on the TV to watch cartoons. "Next week do I have to go back to school?"

"Yes, you have to go back to school." Rick had called the school and told them of the horrible accident and that Trisha would not be back until next week. He also called his boss and asked if he could take his vacation time now, explaining he needed some time to himself. His boss was very understanding and told him to go ahead. He knew when he went back to work, Mary would watch Trisha before and after school. The phone rang, interrupting his thoughts.

"Hi, I was wondering if I could come by and pick up Trisha. My mother wants to take her shopping. She thinks it would be good to get her out of the house. Is that okay with you?" Loretta asked.

Rick rubbed his forehead. The aspirins finally took his headache away. "I think that would be a good idea. I might be asleep when you come by so I'll leave the door open."

"Okay, I should be there in an hour." Loretta said good-bye and hung up the phone.

"Aunt Loretta is coming by to take you and grandma shopping. So go up and get ready."

Trisha turned to Rick and pressed her lips together. "Okay," she said, getting up and leaving the room.

Rick did not want to see Loretta when she came by, so he went to his room until he heard the doorbell ring and watched her pull out of the driveway with Trisha.

Chapter Thirty seven

Months had gone by since Connie died. Christmas had been difficult for everyone. Rick did not bother with a tree. New Year's Eve was worse. Mary had taken Trisha for the weekend and Rick stayed home with a bottle of vodka. If he was not drinking he was working. He spent ten, twelve hours a day there. It helped him from thinking about Connie. Once he was home, the loneliness would seep into his heart. He began drinking at night to help him sleep. Loretta came over once a week to clean and spend time with Trisha. Rick made sure he wasn't there on those days. They had gotten into a huge fight recently about his drinking and how he was ignoring Trisha. He knew she was right, but for now it was the only way he could handle difficult situations. He did his best in the mornings getting Trisha ready before taking her to Mary's. Nothing he did seem to please Mary. One evening after work when he went to pick up Trisha, Mary insisted she have a word with him.

"She really thinks she's having a conversation with Connie." Mary said, looking out the kitchen window to be sure Trisha was out of hearing range. "I really think she needs to see a counselor. If you don't take her, I will." Mary stood at the kitchen sink with her arms crossed, showing her aggravation.

Rick sat down at the table. "Let me talk to her first. I thought by now this would have stopped." Rick ran his hand through his hair. The long hours at work and his drinking at night were getting to him. He always felt tired or hung over.

Mary walked over to the table and sat down in the chair. Her voice softened showing her sympathy. "I know how hard all of this has been for you. But she needs help. She can't handle it on her own. Look at yourself, Rick. You're an adult and having a difficult time. Can you imagine being only seven and feeling this stress?"

"Okay, Mary," Rick said. "I'll look into it." Rick knew Trisha's fantasies were getting out of hand. More and more Trisha would bring up something that she insisted her mother had told her recently. The conversation ended as Trisha skipped into the room.

"Get your things together so we can go home." Rick said, getting up from the chair and following her into the hallway. "Thanks a lot, Mary; I'll see you Monday." Rick opened the front door.

"Bye grandma," Trisha said giving her a kiss on the cheek.

"Bye, and you don't forget to do your homework." Mary said, hugging Trisha. She watched as Rick and Trisha pulled out of the driveway and waved before closing the door.

"Did you eat?" Rick asked Trisha as he pulled into the same fast food restaurant he always stopped.

"Yes, grandma made me ham and potatoes. I told grandma you like to eat here often. She said you should learn how to cook."

"Grandma should learn to mind her own business." Rick thought as he looked over at Trisha. Her long black silky hair and her sharp blue eyes were the same as Connie's. Each day she grew more to look like her.

"May I take your order?" a young girl's voice came from the box.

Rick stated his order and pulled up to the window, paid the girl and took the bag from her hand and headed for home. It was nearly dark as they pulled into the driveway. No one greeted them as they entered the house. Connie's cat Misty died years before. Rick had wanted to surprise her with another before that awful night. He put the food down on the counter as Trisha went into the living room and turned on the TV. Rick finished his meal and threw the paper in the trash. He took a glass from the cabinet and reached under the sink for his bottle of vodka and walked into the living room to his chair. Now he could let himself become numb. Trisha was sitting on the floor when she glanced at him and quickly turned her attention back to the screen. He poured himself another glass and soon his thoughts turned to Connie. His arms longed to hold her, to feel her body next to his, to feel her tender touch, her sweet smell, her voice. God, how he missed her. His mind replayed the conversation with Mary. He told her he would find a counselor. Loretta's face popped into his head. Last time she came by she let him know she felt tired of watching him destroy his life and Trisha's with his self-pity and drinking. He felt everyone was ganging up on him. He had a right to be miserable. "Why can't they just leave me alone?" he mumbled.

Trisha looked up from the TV. "What did you say?"

"I said why can't your grandmother and everyone else leave me alone?" he slurred.

"Mommy doesn't like to see you like this."

Okay, Rick thought. Two can play this game. "So where is Mommy now?" he asked sarcastically. "Is she sitting in the corner?" Rick turned to where the two walls met. "Connie, you're looking as beautiful as ever. Death hasn't changed you at all. So, how are things on the other side?"

"She is not here now," Trisha said annoyed. "She's probably at Sundown Creek. She told me that was her favorite spot. You know, the place where you and mommy use to go riding."

Rick jumped up from his chair knocking over his drink. He grabbed Trisha by the arms and began to shake her hard. "When are you going to stop this nonsense?" he yelled as his face turned red. "You know mommy's dead and she's not coming back. I'm sick of this game you're playing; do you understand me?" Seeing Trisha's tears streaming down her shocked face made Rick stop. "Oh my God, what have I done?" Rick asked as he went back to his chair. Trisha ran from the room, sobbing. "Oh baby, I'm so sorry," Rick said after she left. He held his head in his hands and cried.

.

Chapter Thirty eight

Trisha could not stop her tears as she retrieved her suitcase from her closet and laid it on her bed. She went to her dresser, pulled open the top drawer and began packing what she thought she needed. Rick does not want me, she thought. Just as my real dad does not want me. She had asked Rick one night when he was drunk if he knew anything about her real father.

"I am your father," he told her.

"I mean the other one," she asked.

"He's someone famous and doesn't have time for you. And don't ask me anymore questions."

"If only I knew who and where he was," Trisha thought. Then I could go there. Maybe mommy will tell me. Trisha wiped her tears. That's it. I will go to Sundown Creek and ask her. She continued to pack what would fit into her bag. She then tiptoed down the stairs into the living room to see if Rick was asleep. She saw the TV was still on and could hear his heavy breathing. She knew he probably would not wake up until morning. She quietly went back to her room and grabbed her suitcase and went out the front door. It was so dark out. "I should not be out after dark," she thought. "This is really important. I have to go to Sundown Creek. I have to find my mom."

Chapter thirty nine

Rick awoke with the familiar throbbing in his head. He was not surprised to find he had slept in the chair all night with the TV on. He reached for the remote and shut it off. He looked over at the clock on the mantle that read ten thirty. He got up from the chair and stretched. He then went into the kitchen and made some coffee. As he grabbed for a couple of aspirins, he wondered why Trisha was not down to watch her usual Saturday morning cartoons. The memory of losing his temper and shaking her came back. "Oh, man," he said loudly. "She's still probably upset with me." He put down his cup of coffee on the table and went upstairs to her room. The door was wide open and her bed looked as if it had not been slept in all night. He looked around the room and saw one of her drawers was open and empty. "Trisha!" he called. When there was no answer Rick began to panic. He opened a few more drawers and her closet. Most of them were empty.

That confirmed his suspicions. She had run away. He sat on her bed in disbelief. "Think," he said loudly. "Where would she go?" Mary's, he thought. Maybe Trisha called her last night and she came and picked her up. His heartbeat began to slow down as he went into his bedroom to call. He let the phone ring several times before hanging up the receiver. Maybe they were outside. He quickly threw on some clean clothes and grabbed his keys and drove over to Mary's. When he pulled in the driveway he knew no one was home. He sat in the car hoping Mary would show up with Trisha. His mind kept flashing back to the previous night. "It was so wrong of me to lose my temper like that," he thought. "I have to get my head together before I lose Trisha for good. She is all that I have now. How could I treat her so badly?" Her words came back to him. Mommy's probably at Sundown Creek. Rick suddenly knew in his heart that is where Trisha went. He started his car and headed out of town. The throbbing in his head intensified. What time did Trisha leave the house? Was she out all night? It would have taken almost the whole night just to walk there. He had to get there as soon as possible. Rick increased his speed. He left a dusty trail behind him as he turned down the dirt road leading to the ranch. He parked his car and approached one of the ranch hands that worked there.

"I need a horse; can you saddle one up for me?"

The young man squinted as he looked at Rick. "Okay, I was just getting one ready. He disappeared into the barn and returned with a dark brown horse fully saddled and ready to go.

Rick took the reigns from the man and thanked him. He mounted the horse and headed out towards Sundown Creek. Rick urged the horse to go faster and narrowly missed a branch to his face. Soon he came to the familiar clearing and stopped. He eyes searched the fields for Trisha. He then spotted her under a nearby tree, not moving. Again panic over came him as he dismounted from the horse and ran towards her. Trisha!" Rick said loudly as he neared her. He felt relief when she opened her eyes startled.

"Rick!" Trisha said, rubbing the sleep from her eyes. "How did you know where I was?"

He grabbed her and held her tight. "I was so worried when I found you gone. Don't ever do this to me again, promise."

"I didn't think you wanted me anymore." Trisha's tears came to her eyes. "But mommy said I was wrong. She told you where to find me, didn't she?"

A cool breeze passed as Rick looked over to the spot where he and Connie had once made love. There he saw her, standing under the willow tree, a white glow surrounding her as she smiled. He could not remember when he saw her more beautiful. He could not take his eyes off her as he watched her long hair blowing in the wind. In his heart he knew she wanted him to remember the promise he made to her, the promise to take care of Trisha. He swallowed hard as tears came to his eyes remembering the promise he had almost broken and the love he would always have for Connie. "I will," he whispered. "I will." He watched as she slowly lifted her arm to wave good-bye as she faded away. His eyes looked down at Trisha as she layed in his arms and gently squeezed her. "Come on, let's go home."

THE END

SOMEONE TO LOVE

WOLFCLOUD BOOKS

About the Author

Dawn Scala was raised in a small town in Algonquin Illinois. Her father was a well known musician in the Chicago area. She is currently working on a fiction novel with Tony Seda. Her hobbies include reading and writing and genealogy.

www.ingramcontent.com/pod-product-compliance
Lightning Source LLC
Chambersburg PA
CBHW060820120626

46557CB00001B/297